The Past Never Dies

P.C. JAMES

VINCI
BOOKS

By P.C. James

Miss Riddell Cozy Mysteries

For my family. The inspiration they provide and the time they allow me for imagining and typing makes everything possible.

Vinci Books

vinci-books.com

Published by Vinci Books Ltd in 2026

1

Copyright © P.C. James 2022

A CIP catalogue record for this book is available from the British Library.
Paperback ISBN: 9781036707606

The EU GPSR authorised representative is Logos Europe, 9 rue Nicolas
Poussion, 17000 La Rochelle, France
contact@logoseurope.eu

Chapter One

NORTHUMBERLAND, ENGLAND

January 1954

WHEN SHE HEARD on the radio that the Lindisfarne Gospels were coming to Durham Cathedral, Pauline Riddell was sewing armor inside her coat and hat. Not real armor, of course, just leather, wool padding, and anything else that might soften a blow or stop a knife. She'd already tried on the wide leather dog collar she hoped would prevent strangulation. She needed to be safe for the next, and she hoped final, part of her investigation into the two apparent suicides in the quiet village of Mitford.

Her bedroom window thumped as a blast of wintry sleet was slammed against it. She looked up at the window and shivered. The small two-bar electric fire in her room barely raised the room's temperature and ice patterns were forming on the inside of the window. It was a typical January day in northern England. Pauline returned to her work.

The radio she'd bought herself was playing the latest

songs, helping to pass the time, while her hands kept busy with her sewing. One song particularly caught her attention. It was popular right then; Burl Ives singing *I knew an Old Lady Who Swallowed a Fly*. It seemed apt and made her smile sadly. The old lady who'd written asking for Pauline's help hadn't swallowed a fly, or any of the other animals in the silly song, but she had died nevertheless.

On the hour, the news was announced. It told the usual litany of horrors interspersed with some lighter, human stories designed to stop a sensitive person switching off. Pauline listened with only half her attention, until the announcer said, "In a joint statement today, the British Museum and the office of the Bishop of Durham have agreed on a loan of the Lindisfarne Gospels to Durham Cathedral during a two-week-long event to celebrate the life of St. Cuthbert, whose body is interred in the cathedral."

The announcer moved on to the weather leaving Pauline again unsure she'd heard what she'd heard. A priceless national treasure from the Anglo-Saxon period, which had been kept solely in the British Museum in London for centuries, was going to be on display here in the north. She laid aside her sewing and went downstairs to ask if the Bertrams, whose house she lodged in, had heard the announcement.

They had and Mrs. Bertram was as excited as Pauline to think they could visit something so unique. An artifact that originated from the north, going back almost to the beginning of Christianity here in the north of England, would for a brief time return to the north.

The local newspapers the following day all had articles on the event, with scheduled dates when the book of the four gospels would be open for viewing, and what this happy occasion was to be in aid of. The magnificence of the event, it seemed, had mundane roots. The cathedral, which had stood for nearly a thousand years, needed repair, particularly the roof, and the event was to raise funds. And, it was thought, the event would lift the local population's spirits, who were not as happy as might have been expected after nearly a decade of peace.

Pauline and Mrs. Bertram agreed to buy tickets and visit as soon as they could. Then, at church on Sunday, they were provided an even more blessed result. Local churches from Durham, Northumberland, and Cumberland, were invited to take part in services that would be held during this period of pilgrimage and prayer.

"I shall do both," Pauline said suddenly, as they walked back from church. "I'll go with the church and also as a member of the public. To see a relic of this kind almost in its original setting is an opportunity not to be missed."

"The public tickets are quite expensive, dear," Mrs. Bertram said seriously.

"The Gospels will return to the museum in London and will only be seen along with a thousand other relics," Pauline said. "There's no joy in that. It would cost me a lot more to take a train to London and see the book there. It will be money well spent to see the Gospels in the great cathedral where it belongs."

"To see it in Durham Cathedral and at the tomb of St. Cuthbert," Mr. Bertram said, "will be wonderful indeed. I think it should also spend time on the Holy Island of Lindisfarne, where it was created by our forebears."

"Hardly our ancestors," Pauline said. "Monks were celibate."

"Their brothers and sisters had children," Mr. Bertram said, smiling, "and that's how we're here, so I maintain my statement. Maybe they weren't direct ancestors, but they were family nonetheless."

Pauline laughed. "I can see this visit of the Gospels is going to cause lively discussion for the next week until it arrives and maybe even after it's returned to London."

"So long as the discussions are happy and lively," Mr. Bertram said. "Then it will be a good thing. It's time the practice of having everything held in London and the rest of us do without was talked about."

Pauline felt a flicker of unease. If someone as conventional as Mr. Bertram was wondering if things in England were badly arranged, could there be others less conventional thinking the same? She shook her head. *What nonsense you do think sometimes, Pauline*, passed quickly through her mind.

The local newspapers printed, and BBC radio talked, a lot about the coming event in the days that followed. There were times the BBC's invited expert's words grated on Pauline's sensibilities. Listening to one discussion, Pauline got the strong impression the museum was gifting the Gospels to savages, rather than returning the book to where it had been created thirteen hundred years before.

When Ted Watson was finally arrested for both Mitford murders (and the story written up in wild overstatement by her reporter friend Poppy in an article titled, *Then There Were... Two Murders?*) Pauline's spirits, which had soared during the unraveling of the puzzle, crashed: the inevitable low after the emotional high of the successful outcome. As the days passed, her attention turned once more to the upcoming exhibition of the Lindisfarne Gospels.

As she usually did when confronting something new, especially something she knew so little about, Pauline retired to the local library each evening and read everything they had on the subject. As she read, she began to share some of Mr. Bertram's feelings about where this relic should reside. It made her feel slightly ashamed and then angry. Would she be so ignorant about this artifact if it had been on display here, where it was created? Wouldn't she and every other northern schoolchild have been taken to see it if it had been here rather than on display far away in London?

What she learned was The Lindisfarne Gospels was a single book of the four gospels, hand copied from earlier gospels by monks on the island of Lindisfarne, ever since then known as Holy Island, off Northumberland's coast. This book of the four gospels brought together in one volume with intricately woven, colorful stylized symbolic creatures, was considered one of the country's finest examples of Dark Age culture. Beautifully inscribed with great care by those Anglo-Saxon monks around the year 700 AD, it was a remarkable example of the skill of craftsmen during darker days. Down the centuries, the Gospels had survived raids by Vikings (only just) and Scots, the Reformation of the church in England and the overthrow of Catholicism, the dissolution of monasteries by Henry VIII, the English Civil War and, after their removal to London in the 17th Century, the recent bombings of London by the Germans.

Thinking this would be something an active reporter like Poppy would be interested in, Pauline phoned Poppy and asked if she would be writing an article on the coming exhibition.

"You must be joking," Poppy said, laughing. "I want to write about the here and now, not about relics."

"But the exhibition is here and now," Pauline replied. "It's getting lots of attention in the rest of the press."

"A lot of attention from old people and weirdos," Poppy

said. "People like you and me don't want this stuff. We want what's new and alive."

Realizing not everyone was as enthusiastic as she'd become about the region's history, Pauline decided to try the question on her colleague in crime, Inspector Ramsay. It seemed he wasn't any more enthusiastic than Poppy.

"I'm done with religion, Miss Riddell," he said. "History's a wonderful thing, if you don't have to live in it."

"But the Lindisfarne monastery was founded by Scots out of Iona," Pauline said. "Doesn't that give you a feeling of kinship?"

He laughed. "Iona was begun by Scots right enough, as they were invading out of Ireland. I think I'm a Pict at heart, and not a Scot. Worse, those monks were Catholic missionaries, and my folks are Protestant. That may not mean much here in England, which is why I choose to live here, but it still means a lot in Scotland, Ireland, and Wales. No, I won't be viewing the Gospels, Miss Riddell. I prefer my history to stay dead and buried. It doesn't do to re-awaken old quarrels."

She found Inspector Ramsay's comments as unsettling as Mr. Bertram's had been so Pauline gave up encouraging her friends to take an interest and busied herself with work and planning her own small pilgrimage to see the Gospels.

Fortunately for Pauline, for their rejection stung at the time, Poppy had suggested a celebration of their own. An evening at a pub to celebrate Pauline and Inspector Ramsay's success in the Mitford Murders case, but mainly, in Poppy's mind, to celebrate Poppy's elevation to journalism's higher ranks.

Chapter Two

A NEW PUZZLE

THE CELEBRATION BEGAN with Inspector Ramsay being late. When he arrived, Pauline and Poppy were already settled in the Black Bull's 'snug' room drinking to Pauline's latest success, and Poppy's success in writing and selling the story to Britain's biggest national newspapers.

In Poppy's mind, the wider sales of her articles were the start of a dream. No longer a junior reporter on a small-town provincial paper, she was now a name on papers read around the world. For Pauline, however, this second success in less than a year was a mixture of pride – which she knew was a sin – and trepidation. Poppy's articles, however gratifying, might lead to others seeking her help and she may let them down, something Pauline would never want to do.

"Here he is," Poppy said, seeing Inspector Tom Ramsay making his way from the bar to the small, relatively private room where they were sitting. "You're late, Inspector. We're a drink ahead of you. You'll have to buy us a second, for you can't drink yours alone."

Ramsay smiled. "What are you having?" he asked,

before taking their order back to the bar and returning a few minutes later with their drinks on a tray.

"It's ungentlemanly to keep a lady waiting," Poppy said. "Keeping two waiting is unforgivable."

"Unfortunately, something came up at work and I had to stay and set the team in motion," he said. "Cheers!" He lifted his glass and they responded in kind.

"Anything in my line, Inspector?" Poppy asked eagerly.

Ramsay shook his head. "Not yet," he said, "but there may be something for Miss Riddell to ponder."

"Why can't the press be told?" Poppy demanded. "Is it about last night's bank robbery in Durham?"

"It might be but there's no story yet," Ramsay said. "It's just a small matter I'd like an outside opinion on, that's all."

"And you think I can help, Inspector?" Pauline asked, puzzled. "Tell me."

"Later, Miss Riddell," Ramsay said. "Today we're celebrating your success."

Pauline flushed pink and Ramsay laughed.

"You're blushing, Pauline," Poppy teased her.

"I'm not used to having my praises quite so publicly sung," Pauline said.

"Then we'll never mention them again," Ramsay said, grinning. "That way you'll be sure to know how highly you're regarded."

"To Pauline," Poppy said, raising her glass. "Our very own Miss Marple."

As they left the pub, Poppy went to the toilet. Pauline and Ramsay waited in the pub doorway, unwilling to go out into the cold, damp, evening air. The Inspector took the opportunity of Poppy's absence to say, "Please phone me at this number, Miss Riddell." He handed her a page torn

8

from a notepad. "It's my home phone because I'd like to talk privately."

"What is this about, Inspector?" Pauline asked, faintly concerned this was exactly what she'd feared. She was getting in above her head.

"Later, Miss Riddell," he replied.

Poppy joined them outside, looking at each of them searchingly trying to guess what they'd been saying without her.

"I must go," Ramsay called over his shoulder, walking back to his car. "Good night to you both. I'm sure we'll meet again."

The two young women walked to Poppy's flat with Poppy questioning Pauline every step of the way.

"Enough, Poppy," Pauline said, when they'd reached Poppy's flat, and her car. "Inspector Ramsay hasn't told me anything and even if he had, I wouldn't break his confidence. Thank you for these newspaper clippings." She took them from her bag and put them in the car. "I'll treasure them. The high point, and end, of my career as a sleuth."

"Nonsense," Poppy said. "He's already asking for more help. You're going places my girl, whether you like it or not."

Pauline laughed. "I'd be a real biblical Jonah if more murders were to come my way, wouldn't I? See you soon, Poppy." She leapt in the car and drove away, wondering how she could show the Bertrams the newspaper stories without appearing to boast about them. She decided it would be best just to show them and not worry about appearances. Pride may come before a fall but she hadn't yet agreed to take part in any new investigation so it couldn't be that big of a fall.

Chapter Three

THE GOSPELS ARE MISSING

THE BERTRAMS WERE SO excited by Poppy's newspaper articles printed in the national press; even Mr. Bertram sounded impressed. Poppy was, after all, their niece and family. Pauline found it hard to get away from them to phone Inspector Ramsay until almost bedtime.

"Miss Riddell," he said, when she'd told him who was calling. "You've decided it might be interesting, I guess."

Pauline explained about the Bertrams' determination to hear everything about the murders and how she'd found the killer.

"You must get used to being a celebrity," Ramsay said. "Everybody's wild about amateur detectives nowadays. Even here in the far north, we're constantly told how Wimsey, or Poirot, or Miss Marple would have an answer in an hour when we've been working for days."

"I'm sure it must be very irritating for you," Pauline said. "Do you think the public knows these characters aren't real and the solutions of the imaginary crimes are already determined before the author sits down to write?"

"I'm sure they do but they struggle to connect the dots," Ramsay said. "Now, can I be confident you won't share with anyone what I'm about to tell you? If you can't swear this on your bible, I will end this call now."

"I swear, Inspector," Pauline said. "And that means something to me."

"The Lindisfarne Gospels are missing."

"What?" Pauline cried. "I have tickets to see them." He'd said missing, but that meant stolen, for it couldn't be anything else. You don't accidentally mislay such a treasure.

Inspector Ramsay continued, "Tonight's news will announce there's been a problem with dampness on the parchment. You will hear that a conservator is coming from the British Museum in London to inspect the book and say if it's safe for them to continue being on display. It isn't true but we hope it will buy enough time to recover the book. He will, of course, be bringing a copy of the book to go back on display so everything looks is as it should do."

"The Gospels only arrived a few days ago," Pauline said. "How could someone develop and carry out a plan to steal them in such a short period of time? It was only last weekend I heard on the radio about the security in place to protect such a national treasure from harm."

"There was a lot of security," Ramsay said. "Clearly, though, not enough. They went missing overnight and, as I'm now free from our recent Mitford entanglements, I've been seconded to the team. This is so important to the authorities some Scotland Yard high-flyer has come up to take charge."

"And they want me to help?"

"No, Miss Riddell. *I'd* like your help. Unofficially, of course," Ramsay said. "But then this whole investigation is unofficial for the Gospels aren't missing, you see."

"Then how are you investigating?" Pauline asked, puzzled.

"I'm working on the real bank robbery that took place on the same night," Ramsay said. "The rest of the team is looking into an art robbery that took place about two weeks ago at one of our local great houses, which allows them to sound out people for a possible religious artifact that might come on the market."

"I can't see how I can help, Inspector," Pauline said, frowning. "This will be just police work, surely."

"You're a churchgoer," Ramsay said. "This is a religious artifact of your church. You might hear talk that I, as a lapsed-Presbyterian atheist, might not. You have a talent for thinking broadly about problems, rather than following trails, as we police are expected to do. I think you would be a useful addition to the team, even if the team doesn't know you're there."

"Seems to me we're both likely to get into terrible trouble if my involvement were to become known."

"It's a risk I'm prepared to take," Ramsay said. "Are you?"

Pauline weighed up the likely repercussions if her involvement became known and they seemed small compared to his before saying, "Well, I won't be able to use my ticket until the Gospels are found. Where do we start?"

"We should meet and talk," Ramsay said. "On my salary, I can't afford long phone calls."

"I can drive into town," Pauline said.

"I'd prefer out of town, in case we're seen by someone who knows me," Ramsay said. "Why not the Ridley Arms in Stannington? It's a long time since I've been there, and it isn't so far for you to drive."

"Very well. Tomorrow is Saturday. I finish work at twelve. Shall we say one o'clock?"

"I'll be there," he said. "We can talk more freely in person." He grinned as he hung up the phone. Some things couldn't be shared, even in person. Like his boss saying, as he'd sent Ramsay off to join the newly formed, and pompously titled, Artefacts Recovery Team. 'Keep them on the straight and narrow, Ramsay. I don't want any big city behavior spoiling our relationship with the public. I'm relying on you.'

"Yes, sir," Ramsay had dutifully replied but felt there'd be little he could do as one among thirty or more other senior and junior officers. And it was in Durham, not Newcastle, so his influence would be small. Even the local officers would view him as a rival rather than a colleague.

His foreboding was proven correct. As Ramsay, like others brought in from the surrounding forces, listened to the very first Team briefing in silence, he contemplated the personal dynamics in the room. The London men were a tight knit group, as you'd expect when a small band is in what they considered hostile territory. The larger group were the local Durham police. They were also tight knit, mainly in opposition to the group who'd been brought in to lead the investigation. Their attention was steady and their manner passively aggressive. They'd do what they were told, and you could be sure they'd do no more.

The rest of the team were isolated individuals, like himself, sent to take part by bosses who wanted a finger in the pie. He and they couldn't be considered a group because, though they had numbers, they barely knew each other and had no history in common. In fact, Ramsay thought, the Recovery Team was the usual bunch of men brought together by circumstances beyond their control and from which they could hope for little gain. Ramsay only hoped in his case there'd be nothing lost either for while his superiors smiled and congratulated him on his recent successes, he felt how much they deplored the reason for them. Civilians were as much the enemy as criminals were, in too many of his bosses' minds.

Chapter Four

SIR ROBERT LAURISTON

FINISHING HIS BREAKFAST, Sir Robert took his coffee to an easy chair that looked out onto the garden where his morning paper was waiting for him. It was his daily routine, and his staff were careful to ensure nothing disturbed it. It wasn't that he was a demanding master. They just shared his taste for an ordered life. If something out of the ordinary were to happen, the staff would be more upset than Sir Robert.

The news was grim as always. The country really wasn't recovering from the war as they'd all hoped. The heart had gone out of it somehow, he thought, as he read of shortages, rationing, strikes, closures, delays, and the general dreariness of poverty around what had once been a prosperous land. Really, it could hardly be worse if they'd lost the war, he thought bitterly. Shaking his head in disgust, he put aside the national newspaper and picked up the local one.

The shock of its headline was almost physical. Harry

Common was dead. Killed in a pub brawl in Durham. He couldn't believe it. What had gone wrong and why?

Sir Robert rose and walked quickly to the bell rope to summon his butler. When he arrived, Sir Robert said, "Did you see this?" He pointed at the headline.

"I did, sir. It's terrible news."

"I must visit Mrs. Common," Sir Robert said. "She must be heartbroken."

"I believe she's staying with friends at present," his butler said. "I can make enquiries where that might be."

"Yes, do that. And when she might return home. It might be better to wait until then for I'll be sure to be in everyone's way if she's with friends."

"I will ascertain if your visit should be immediate or later," the butler replied. "Will this affect your recent work with Mr. Common, sir?"

Sir Robert shook his head. "No, that's all done. I hope what has happened had nothing to do with that."

"Your attendance at the Conservative Club tonight may shed light on that," the butler suggested.

"If I could be sure the Chief Constable would be there, it might."

"I could make enquiries, sir."

Sir Robert nodded. "Yes, do. If not, I'll find some pretext to phone him. After all, Harry Common is one of my tenants. I have a right to know." He lapsed into thoughtful silence.

The butler left the room to begin his research and Sir Robert returned to his chair. Outside a steady rain had begun and he could no longer even see the far end of the garden. It was a rotten day in every sense of the word.

Chapter Five

PAULINE AGREES TO HELP

AS THEY'D ARRANGED, Pauline made her way to the Ridley Arms straight from work. She took a corner seat away from the few other customers. Even Saturday afternoons weren't busy times for country pubs in winter. Ramsay joined her a few minutes later with his pint of bitter.

"You know I can only help after work and at weekends," Pauline said when they'd settled.

"Then if the Gospels are recovered quickly," Ramsay said, "little of your time will have been wasted. If this goes on for weeks, your time will be well spent. We shall never know which it is until after. Much of life is like that, don't you find?"

"I'm too young to have that experience," Pauline said, smiling. "Now tell me everything and I'll start thinking."

"You'll know of the St. Cuthbert event at Durham Cathedral and the Lindisfarne Gospels being loaned from the British Museum to be the center piece of the ceremonies. I'm sure everyone does, there's been so much advertising."

Pauline nodded. "As I said, I was looking forward to seeing them tomorrow and my church was to take part in a service in memory of St. Cuthbert at the cathedral next Sunday. Not just my church, almost every church for fifty miles around was to be there at some time over the coming weeks."

"And you'll still see them, Miss Riddell," Ramsay said. "Or at least a very good copy, which has been brought up from the museum to buy some time while we recover the original."

"It won't feel the same to me," Pauline said, disappointed.

He laughed. "Have you seen the original?"

"No," Pauline said.

"Then you won't know the difference. In fact, according to the experts, even if you have seen the original, you wouldn't be able to tell the difference."

"It will go on display today?" Pauline asked.

Ramsay shook his head. "The story is the conservator is doing tests and won't be able to say yea or nay right away. The plan is to return it to public viewing on Sunday for the previously planned church services."

"Our church was to take part next Sunday," Pauline said. "I hope we have the original back for it. Even if I won't know the difference, I still won't feel right about it."

Ramsay grinned. "I expect I'd feel the same if it were me. It is odd when you think about it. Even experts often can't tell great art works from forgeries and yet we're upset about the forgery. It shouldn't matter but even to an old cynic like myself, it still does."

"Philosophy aside, Inspector," Pauline said, "please continue with what happened."

Nodding, Ramsay said, "Durham police and the British Museum were providing security guards whenever the book was taken from the bank vault to the display case and also on the return."

"I heard that on the radio," Pauline said.

"Well, the Gospel book arrived at Durham last Saturday and was taken straight to the cathedral. It was placed in its display case to confirm it fitted properly and then taken to a local bank vault, Lowther's Bank, for safekeeping," Ramsay explained.

"Was there a guard on the vault all night?" Pauline asked.

"This is Durham we're talking about, Miss Riddell," Ramsay said, "not that den of iniquity, London."

"So that's a no," Pauline said, frowning. "Go on."

"Next morning, the Gospels in their carrying case returned to the cathedral where academics and local dignitaries could see them and talk to the custodians without meeting the public," Ramsay said. "You know the kind of thing, everyone formally dressed, cocktails, the press gathering details for articles and photos. They were in all that night's newspapers. Even the BBC had a camera crew in attendance so the people who have TV could see the party. That evening, the book went back to the vault in its traveling case."

"Was the case fastened to the wrist of one of the guards?" Pauline asked. "I've seen that done in the cinema."

"Again, no. It wasn't thought necessary," Ramsay said. "This is a priceless ancient artifact but only of value to a very small number of collectors or religious people. It wasn't thought to have much significance to the usual criminal."

"A collector of significant artifacts or a religious collector might not agree, Inspector."

"I imagine the team who devised the precautions would agree with you right now, Miss Riddell," Ramsay said. "Anyway, to return to the events. The following day, that was Tuesday, the public access to view the book began. Lines of paying customers filed past the display case as had been hoped, and everything went as expected. In the evening, following the same route and procedure, the book was returned to the bank vault. However, you will learn there were growing protests outside the cathedral throughout the day, which gave the press something exciting to write about. They interviewed and published the protestors' complaints, desires, and other tedious whining."

"I'll need copies of all of those articles, Inspector," Pauline said. "They may be a good place to start."

"I have copies in my car," Ramsay said. "I'll give them to you when we leave."

"Were there protesters at the bank?" Pauline asked.

"No, their activity centered around the cathedral," Ramsay replied. "The following day, everything also went as planned. The Gospels were viewed at the cathedral and returned to the vault. That was Wednesday. Everything went well on Thursday too. Then, disaster. On Friday morning, the carrying case was removed from the vault and taken to the cathedral over the usual route, with the usual guards, and when it arrived, the case was opened, and the Gospels were missing."

"And that was the same night there was a bank robbery in Durham?" Pauline said thoughtfully. "When the radio newsreader said that my heart skipped a beat. I thought at once of the Gospels. Then he said it was Martin's Bank and I relaxed. There was a whole piece on the radio last weekend telling us all the Gospels were being kept at Lowther's Bank. I didn't think broadcasting that was wise but now I know how efficient Poppy is at rooting out information, I took it as just how things are in the world of the press."

Ramsay nodded. "It wasn't wise, and it was that night. It's too much of a coincidence that both banks were robbed on the same night. We think robbing Martin's was intended as a distraction. The robbers used explosives to open that vault, set off the alarm and generally took the police focus away from Lowther's Bank and directed it to Martin's Bank where, by the way, they stole the payroll of one of our biggest local companies. I'm leading the team looking into that angle."

"Was there any additional security on the Lowther Bank at night?"

"The local bobby on the beat was asked to check in on the bank more regularly, and more thoroughly, than he would normally do but beyond that, no. The weakest links were always considered the transfers between the bank and the cathedral."

"A reasonable assumption, I'm sure," Pauline said, "but this is a priceless artifact, and someone would want it for their collection."

Ramsay grimaced. "It's the peculiar nature of its value that's the issue. It isn't a great painting or a great jewel or any of the usual artsy items rich people collect. In this country, religious articles aren't a big attraction the way they might be on the continent."

"You mentioned protesters, Inspector," Pauline said. "Who are they?"

"About a dozen people in each of three different groups. Poverty activists, led by a local trade union firebrand; religious nuts, led by a dotty Catholic woman who wants all the buildings seized by Henry VIII in 1536 returned to the Roman Catholic Church; and a group we'd never even heard of, Northern England nationalists, demanding home rule for the North-East and a return of all the treasures stolen from the north."

"I've heard of Scottish, Welsh, and Irish nationalists but I didn't know we had northern English nationalists," Pauline said, puzzled.

"Nor did any of us," Ramsay said, "which makes them the most suspicious of the three, in my mind."

"There is a lot of bad feeling in the north, though," Pauline said. "It wouldn't surprise me if there weren't calls for some kind of regional government, similar to the calls from Scottish and Welsh Nationalists."

"Agreed," Ramsay said. "Still, it's an interesting coincidence that such a group has emerged just before a priceless artifact from the north should go missing."

"Does that mean the police are focusing on them?"

"Starting there, certainly," Ramsay said. "But not convinced that's where the trail ends. To be honest, they look and sound like a lot of crackpots. The sort who go tramping over the moors and mountains every summer and bore their neighbors and coworkers with stories about the delights of nights spent under the stars."

Pauline laughed. "You're not a camping man then, Inspector?"

He shook his head. "I'm not. A glass of Scotch whisky and my own fireside are just fine for me."

"I feel my best contribution will be with the lady's

church group and those hikers, Inspector. Is that your opinion also?"

"It is, Miss Riddell," Ramsay said. "And even the local union men. You work in industry. You'd have a connection there too."

"The gap between the offices and the shop floor is a wide one, Inspector," Pauline said. "And between the executive suite, where I spend my humble working hours, is even larger. I could get murdered nosing around there, not literally, of course."

Ramsay laughed. "It's in no one's best interests for a murder here. Even stealing priceless national treasures isn't yet a hanging offence."

"Maybe," Pauline said, ruefully remembering her unpleasant encounters with the young factory worker she'd thought had killed Marjorie Armstrong, "but I'll still leave those to last, if you don't mind."

"Then you'll help," Ramsay said. "I'm so glad. I feel you'll get further with those protesters than we would, and I have a strong suspicion they're involved in some way, or some of them are anyway. Even if they don't understand they were involved."

"I don't want to sound as if I'm treating the church women lightly, Inspector. I help at my local church too, but do you really think they could be involved? The women at my home church and the one I attend here are everyday folk. They don't have burgling skills."

Ramsay laughed. "Your question is a fair one, though many might say different, and in this case, they'd be right. Our first inclination was to think it unlikely. Where would they have learned how to do any of the things that happened that night?"

"What changed your minds?"

"The leader of the women up there at the cathedral served in the Special Operations Executive during the war. She was a trainer of underground agents and was twice flown into France to liaise with the Resistance," Ramsay said. "She has the skills, all right. Did she use them? That's what we need to know."

"That is unusual," Pauline said. "What will the police be focusing on while I'm following the trail of protesters?"

"We're following a number of avenues," Ramsay said. "As there's no evidence the Lowther Bank was broken into, let alone robbed, that must mean the security guards, or the manager and under-manager are our most likely villains because only they had keys to the door and the vault. They all seem to be respectable people but there's a team looking at the bank. Who could get in and out without leaving a trace? Then there's a team looking at known handlers of stolen goods and particularly art works. I and my team are looking at that other bank robbery. We have enough to keep ourselves busy, you see."

Pauline frowned as she thought of what she'd just learned. "Inspector, I'm sure the team has thought of this, but the security guards wouldn't know who owned which safety deposit box, nor would they have keys. Only the managers and maybe some staff would know that and have access to any master keys."

"They're looking into all the options, Miss Riddell, you can be sure."

"I'm sure they are. Now, how do I describe myself to them when I meet the protesters?" Pauline asked, puzzled. She'd hardly heard his reply as this knotty problem circled in her head. "I'm not police and I'm not a private detective. If I were elderly, like Miss Marple, I could just be the old busybody asking questions, but I haven't reached those advanced years yet."

"Your fame will open doors," Ramsay said. "One mention of Miss Riddell and you'll have them eating out of your hand."

"But still, I can't talk to them about the missing Gospels because they aren't missing."

"I've thought of that," Ramsay said. "The day after the disappearance of the Gospels, a young local man died after a fight outside a Durham pub. His death was something of an accident, as you'll see when you read today's papers. He had a bone disease that made his bones brittle. In this case, his skull. He was killed by a punch that wouldn't likely have harmed anyone else."

"I don't see how it helps."

"His name was Harry Common. He was from Weardale and had never been to the pub in Durham before, so far as we know. Also, no one there knew him, but his mother says he went into Durham that night on business. There's something fishy about it, in my mind. It's too close to the two bank robberies. But the Scotland Yard man who heads up the Gospels' team had Harry's death quickly assessed by his right-hand men and they say it's not connected to the theft of the Gospels so he's not wasting our resources on it."

"Deaths on London streets being common enough," Pauline said, grinning for she knew Ramsay's opinion of London.

"Aye, right enough," he replied, grinning. "That's more or less what he said. I thought you could talk to the dead man's mother and use that as a starting point. His mother wants confirmation and so on."

"But if he had no links to the protesters," Pauline said, "it doesn't get me far."

"No direct link that I can see, but he is a member of the metalworkers union which is led locally by the man heading up the poverty action protesters," Ramsay said. "I think that's enough to start a conversation."

"It would be them," Pauline said gloomily. "The protesters I most wanted to avoid."

Ramsay laughed. "The witnesses we want to avoid are usually our instincts telling us they're wrong'uns."

"If I'm also found 'accidentally' dead, Inspector," Pauline said, "I hope you'll remember it was at your prompting and you're suitably sorry."

"I'll wear my best suit at your funeral, Miss Riddell, and dab my eyes with a clean hanky. There does that make you feel better?"

"No. It's a gruesome thought," Pauline said, grimacing. "Particularly the phony tears. I'll start tomorrow after I've read all about these protesters as well as the article about the dead man."

"Don't forget Harry Common's mother. That's your entry point, Miss Riddell."

"You keep giving me all the women to talk to, Inspector," Pauline said.

"If we police have a weakness, it's the lack of women police officers. I'm convinced we'd get on a lot quicker in many cases if we had someone to question the women in a way that was reassuring to them."

"You don't say," Pauline said drily. She paused, before saying, "Do you think she'll have anything that will help us?"

"I do," Ramsay replied. "Harry lost his job when the mine closed and he refused a transfer to another one, which means he was still living with his mother right up to his death and if there's anything to know, she will know it."

"And she's not telling you?"

"I wasn't asked to interview her," Ramsay said. "As I said, the big boys did that before deciding there was no connection to the disappearance of the Gospels and dumped the case back on the local force."

"I see," Pauline said. "You think it is related?"

"Don't you?"

"It could be a coincidence," Pauline said.

"It could be, of course," Ramsay replied. "But it was only a day after the disappearance of the Gospels, and the bank robbery, which was also coincidental. Odd don't you think? Anyway, you speaking to his mother might set my mind at rest. Sadly, I can't now because it's been ruled out of the team's remit. At least, I can't without causing upheavals at the local and the Task Force levels."

"You're a Task Force now?"

"I expect us to be a full invasion-of-Normandy operation before the whole thing is wound down," Ramsay said. His tone was flat, neutral, without any obvious hint of sarcasm.

"Will there be medals?" Pauline asked, smiling.

"There are always medals for those who took no risks and blame those who did," Ramsay said.

"Then I shall save you from risk and interview Mrs. Common, Inspector. *After*, I've taken the measure of the protesters. They seem a much more likely place to start."

Chapter Six

REVISED PLAN

AS PAULINE ATE her evening meal, the phone rang. Before she could leave the table, Mrs. Bertram said, "I'll get it. You finish your dinner."

As it wasn't likely to be for her, Pauline wasn't as irritated as she usually was by Mrs. Bertram's proprietary grip on the phone.

"It's for you, Pauline," Mrs. Bertram said, re-entering the dining room. "It's Inspector Ramsay."

"I just left him an hour ago," Pauline said, hurrying to the phone. "It must be important."

"Good evening, Inspector," she said, after picking up the handset.

"It isn't too important, Miss Riddell," Ramsay, who'd heard her comment, said. "I just called to warn you not to interview protesters tonight."

"I wasn't going to, but why do you say that?"

"It seems not showing the book upset folks as much as showing it did," Ramsay said. "The nationalists and the poverty group think the public is being bilked of its rightful due. We 'bosses' are keeping the goodies for ourselves, apparently, and they're out today protesting in force."

"Really, people are the limit," Pauline said. "The book has resided happily in the British Museum for a hundred years or more and never caused this much trouble. What is wrong with these people?"

"Nothing is wrong with them, Miss Riddell. Their need for attention is being pandered to by the press and media. The opportunity hadn't come their way before."

"I'd planned to meet the protesters tomorrow morning after church," Pauline said. "I thought that may be safer."

"Maybe your need for attention wants to be fed too?"

"No, Inspector, it doesn't," Pauline said, crossly. "And I'll take good care to avoid any reporters or radio and television people I see."

"It may have subsided by tomorrow, because the Gospels will be back on display," Ramsay agreed. "Just be careful, that's all."

"I'm always careful, Inspector, as you know. In fact, I might wear my armored-murderer-trapping outfit to be sure."

He laughed. "It might be an idea at that."

"I'll return to my original schedule of meeting Mrs. Common tomorrow instead," Pauline said. "If you'll give me her address."

He flipped through a file and then read out an address in Weardale, a valley in County Durham to the south and west of Newcastle.

"That's well away from the city of Durham," Pauline said. "Did Harry have a car?"

"No," Ramsay said. "But there's a reasonable bus service through the valley and into the city."

"Still, it's a long way to go for a drink," Pauline said. "Surely, there are pubs closer?"

"Many, Miss Riddell, which is one of the reasons I'm suspicious about his death."

Pauline glanced at the grandfather clock that stood in the hall. "I must go," she said. "I'm still reading through the articles you gave me. Thank you for warning me about the protests. I hope your people can police the cathedral well. It's coming to something when even churches have a police presence."

She hung up and went back to finish her meal under the disapproving eye of Mrs. Bertram, who reminded her the food would now be cold. *Really, she's worse than my mother*, Pauline thought for the millionth time since moving in with her fiancé Stephen's parents, the Bertrams. *I must find a place of my own.* Unfortunately, the difficulty she discovered, each time she decided this, was they'd been so kind when she'd needed support and leaving without a good reason would make her feel ungrateful. Worse, she felt Mrs. Bertram mothered her because she could no longer mother Stephen and that leaving would be a crushing blow to the poor woman.

Throughout the evening and all that night, Pauline's mind ran like a hamster on a wheel with thoughts on the actions of the protesters. Did the increased protests mean they didn't steal the Gospels and they were genuinely in the dark as to why they were not on show? Or was it the opposite, they had stolen them, and this was their way of pretending they hadn't? She was no nearer answering that question when her alarm rang, and she slipped out of bed. She dressed while in a thoughtful mood. Today was Sunday; she would drive straight from church to Mrs. Common's home to begin her investigation.

Chapter Seven

MRS. COMMON

STRAIGHT FROM CHURCH, without stopping for lunch, Pauline drove to the address Inspector Ramsay had given her. It would have been an hour on a good day. On a wintry day, with the slush covered icy roads in Weardale, her pace soon slowed to a crawl. There was little traffic on these narrow country lanes, which lessened her fear of a collision but increased her fear of sliding into a ditch. It would be a long walk back to town for help.

From the steamy car windows, she could see the snow-covered uplands to the south, while the lower ground to her right was shiny wet. A shininess that suggested ice. She shivered, and not just because the Austin's heater wasn't raising the temperature in the car. This was a lonely spot to be stranded. She gripped the wheel tightly and crawled her way to the small village where the Common's cottage was situated.

The village was little more than a pub, a garage that once had been the local blacksmiths, a church that looked abandoned, and four cottages straggling along the roadside. Mrs. Common's cottage was the farthest of the four. Pauline parked, pulled her coat collar up to her ears, her hat down over her ears, and stepped out into the thin sleet that was soaking everything. She walked briskly to the cottage door and knocked.

When the door opened, Pauline noted that Mrs. Common looked older than her years. She could hardly be more than fifty, but her hair was white, and her posture stooped. Grief and a lifetime of hard work would do that to you.

"Mrs. Common?"

"Yes," the woman replied. Her gaze was open, disinterested. As though she neither knew nor cared who came to her door.

"I'm Pauline Riddell. You may have heard of me?"

The woman shook her head.

Disappointed, Pauline tried again. "I had some success in solving three murders recently."

Mrs. Common seemed unimpressed and still said nothing, as though waiting for Pauline to get to the point.

So, Pauline did. "I wanted to talk to you about your son's death," Pauline said. "May I come in?"

The woman nodded and led the way into the cottage. Even though it was midday it was dark inside. Outdoors the low heavy clouds were shutting out most of the sunlight. Inside, the only light came through heavily net-curtained windows. In the living room, a single-bulb light hanging from the center of the ceiling, its brightly patterned lampshade focusing the light down, left the upper corners of the room in darkness.

The furniture, however, was modern, clean, and well-kept. Mrs. Common was house-proud. The table at the window catching the light was cleared of all but a small vase of snowdrops that were reflected in the table's polished surface. Maybe a well-wisher had bought them to cheer up the grieving mother. Pauline wished she'd thought to bring flowers too.

Mrs. Common gestured Pauline to an armchair while she perched on the edge of the couch waiting for Pauline to speak.

"I'm not a reporter," Pauline said, hoping that might set the woman at ease. "I'm someone who searches for the truth in cases where others have given up. May I sit down?"

The woman nodded and pointed again to the armchair, much used and shiny at the arms. Pauline sat. From here, she could see into the cottage's small kitchen where, once again, Mrs. Common's industrious activity was evident. The sink was spotless, the curtain below it hiding the water pipes, and no doubt cleaning aids, was newly laundered. The linoleum floor was polished so that it shone even in the pale sunlight creeping in at the window above the basin.

Pauline had to collect her thoughts, for her inspection of the woman's kitchen had unsettled her, grief expressing itself in so many different ways. "Can you tell me about your son, Harry?"

"Why?"

This was promising. It was only the second word she'd spoken. "Because even if what happened was an accident, someone hit him, and he died."

"Men hit each other all the time," Mrs. Common said, dully. "You can't lock them all up."

Pauline smiled. "I think there may have been more to what happened than just a pub brawl about nothing much."

"Oh."

Pauline waited, hoping something more would come. It didn't. "Wouldn't you like to know what happened and why?"

"Will it bring Harry back?"

"No. It might give you some relief from your pain to understand what happened."

"Have you ever lost someone?"

Pauline hesitated. "Yes, I have."

"Do you know why they died, and does it help you?"

"I don't know exactly," Pauline admitted. "I do know it drives me to explain other deaths in the hope I might help others."

"Oh."

Silence again descended. Pauline began again. "Was The Wheatsheaf in Durham where Harry usually spent his evenings?"

Mrs. Common shook her head.

"It does seem a long way to go for a pint," Pauline said, nodding. "I wondered why he was there. In Durham, I mean, rather than the local pub I saw as I drove into the village."

"He had business," Mrs. Common said.

"Did he say what kind of business?"

"Nay. He said nought to me afore he went."

"You've no idea? What has he been working on lately? Maybe it was something to do with that?"

The old woman shook her head.

"I understand he was one of those laid off when they closed the pit," Pauline said. "That must have been very hard."

"I told them nought good would come of letting the government own the mine," she said, obviously giving an

34

answer she'd given many times before. "It took a while, but the chickens came home to roost with a vengeance."

"I imagine most of the workers thought they'd be better off with the government in charge, rather than an employer who could fire them at will," Pauline said, feeling she was beginning to get the woman to loosen up at last.

"Aye, they did. Bigger fools they," she said. "Sir Robert has always dealt fairly with those that dealt fairly with him. What do people in London know of us or what's best for us?"

"I heard the mine was old with poor coal and narrow seams, which made it too hard to work," Pauline said.

Mrs. Common nodded. "Which is why Sir Robert couldn't pay what the other mine owners paid. We all knew that. The idiots thought somehow they would be paid the same as the other miners while producing little coal of poor quality. Fools. The mine was doomed the moment it was handed over to time-and-motion men."

If she'd talked like this when the mines were being nationalized, and in the years since, she couldn't have been popular in the neighborhood, Pauline surmised. Could that be why Harry died? Did he share her unhappiness?

"But if the mine wasn't able to produce the product the customers wanted, even Sir Robert couldn't have kept it going much longer," Pauline suggested.

"The mine had plenty of customers," Mrs. Common said sharply. "Older people, poorer people, people who couldn't afford a lot of the high-quality coal but could buy enough of our coal to keep themselves warm in winter. You know as little about customers as them that came from London with their big plans and even bigger promises."

"You have a good fire going today," Pauline said brightly. "Do you receive cheap coal from the Coal Board?"

The older woman laughed harshly. "Nay," she said. "This from Sir Robert's other coal seam."

"There were two mines?" Pauline asked.

The woman shook her head. "Only the one seam was being worked because it was the better of the two. When the board took the working one and then shut it down, though they didn't hand it back, he had some of the unemployed lads open this second one. That way we on Sir Robert's estate still get enough coal to keep us alive through the winter. Without it, most of us could barely keep body and soul together round here."

"It's true we have a lot of poor people who haven't recovered from these wars and the earlier Depression," Pauline said. "Did Harry share your views about the mine being nationalized?"

"Aye. He has," she paused, "had more sense than most around here."

"Could that have been what the argument was about?"

"Nay. The mine closed two years ago. The heat has gone out of that. Two years ago, there was trouble. The same men who'd shouted at Harry and me for taking Sir Robert's side against the National Coal Board, then shouted at us because we were proven right." She shook her head. "There's no accounting for folks."

"Was Harry working on anything right now?"

"He was doing metalworking jobs for people in the village," Mrs. Common said. "He was a real craftsman with metal. He could do anything with it; ornaments, monuments, gates, doors, anything you needed. And Sir Robert often found him things to mend or make around the estate. He's been good to us. He let us live on in this cottage, which he didn't need to do. When the mine was taken from him, the workers houses were taken too. All except this cottage."

"He wasn't working on anything for Sir Robert right now?" Pauline tried to make that sound like a harmless question.

Mrs. Common shook her head. Her face creased in concentration for a moment, then she said, "He was making some lunch boxes for some fellow union men, he told me. But they were delivered just before he died."

"Lunch boxes?"

Mrs. Common nodded. "You know the thing. The 'working man's briefcase', Harry called them."

Pauline laughed. "Yes, I see." And for the first time, she thought she did see.

"What did the lunchboxes look like?" Pauline asked. "They must have been special for folks to order bespoke ones."

"I told you, like briefcases," Mrs. Common said. "The lads wanted to make fun of the office workers, see?"

Pauline smiled. "I do see. I work in the offices of a factory, and it would be funny. You don't know who ordered the lunch boxes? Harry didn't keep paperwork of customers and what they paid?"

Mrs. Common laughed, genuinely amused. It brightened her whole demeanor.

"This isn't a shop, lass. We do things for friends, and they do things for us. If money changes hands, it's just in the way of equalizing the trade."

Pauline smiled. "I just hoped it might lead to someone who I could talk to. Were there many lunch boxes? Was it a work gang or a factory shift?"

"Nay, nought like that," Mrs. Common said. "One man ordered one and then his friend liked the sound of it and ordered one as well."

"Two, then," Pauline said. "But you really can't remember Harry mentioning a name?"

'I wouldn't know them anyway," Mrs. Common said. "They weren't local. They were union men from Durham. I remember Harry saying."

"Perhaps I met them at the protest yesterday," Pauline said, untruthfully. "Are you sure you can't remember a name or nickname?"

Mrs. Common shook her head. "Harry never said."

"Did Harry go into Durham to meet the same people?" Pauline asked.

"I don't know."

Pauline smiled. Showing her disappointment wouldn't help. "If anything does come to mind, you will get in touch, won't you?" she said. "I'll give you my telephone number, in case." She wrote out the number on a page from her notebook, tore it out and handed it to Mrs. Common. "Be sure to call after seven in the evening. I'm always in after that time."

"I will," the old woman said. "I can't think of anything right now. It's all just a blur."

"I understand," Pauline said, sympathetically, for she did understand. She could remember feeling lost, detached from life in the weeks after Stephen was killed. "Do you think Sir Robert might know anything about what happened?"

"Nay. I shouldn't think so, but you can ask. He allus has time for regular folk."

"That's good to know," Pauline said. "I'll phone him when I get home and ask for an appointment."

Pauline left the cottage and walked thoughtfully back to the car. Sir Robert's house was just half a mile further up the lane and if he was as amenable as Mrs. Common said, she could save a lot of time by simply driving up to the house and asking. She smiled to herself. Sir Robert may be as affable as Mrs. Common suggested; however, she suspected his butler would guard his master's privacy even harder because of it. She would phone the moment she was home.

Chapter Eight

PAULINE MEETS SIR ROBERT

HER SLOW PROGRESS back the way she'd come showed her how impractical it would be to go home and return here before the light went out of the day. As Pauline neared the more built-up areas between the Tyne and Wear Valleys, she saw a hotel that said its dining room was open. She pulled in and parked.

A server invited her to take a seat. The room was almost empty, and she had a choice of places to sit. Pauline took a table by the window and ordered quickly, asking if there was a phone she could use. With her order underway, and a small glass of sherry waiting, she made her way to the bar where the waiter had promised a phone. She was in luck. Beside the phone, there was a phone book. Pauline found Sir Robert's number and called.

The phone was answered, not by a haughty butler, as she'd expected, but by an efficient sounding woman, which Pauline found even more unsettling though she couldn't say why. She explained who she was and why she needed to speak to Sir Robert.

"I will consult with Sir Robert and let you know, Miss Riddell. Please hold the line."

Pauline hoped she wouldn't be too long; the cost of phone calls was a luxury on her wages. And the hotel would want to be paid for the use of their line as well, she was sure.

"Miss Riddell?" The woman's voice sounded hopeful as though she expected Pauline to have hung up.

"I'm here," Pauline replied.

"Sir Robert could see you this afternoon, if you can be here."

Pauline assured her she could, and they set a time. Hanging up the phone, Pauline went straight to the powder room to freshen her appearance. She splashed her face with water, dried it, and dabbed powder on her nose and cheeks, before returning to her seat. She should have made the appointment for later, she thought as she waited impatiently for her lunch to arrive. After eating, Pauline once again inspected her teeth and reapplied her lipstick. That secretary had sounded judgmental, and Pauline didn't like the idea she might fail to pass the entrance test.

Fortunately, it seemed the secretary didn't answer doors and the man who showed her through into Sir Robert's Conservatory showed no inclination to judge her appearance.

"A Miss Pauline Riddell," the man said, and stood aside to allow Pauline to enter.

"Not 'a' Miss Riddell, Carter, 'the' Miss Riddell." Sir Robert was a tall, well-built man. He was around fifty and still in what people called 'his prime'. His grin, as he spoke to his servant, was broad and genuinely friendly. It encompassed the servant and Pauline in a surprisingly warm greeting.

"Will you take tea, Miss Riddell?" Sir Robert asked.

"Thank you. That would be nice."

"Two teas, please, Carter, and any fancies cook has ready."

"Very good, sir," Carter said, returning to the door, leaving Pauline to accept Sir Robert's vigorous handshake alone.

"There are seats along here," Sir Robert said, leading her deeper into the Conservatory.

Comfortable looking rattan chairs in colonial style were grouped around a small table and looked out through the glass to the wet park beyond. Pauline took the seat Sir Robert held for her and waited for him to sit before saying, "I hope you don't mind this intrusion, but I think you can help me with some enquiries."

"That sounds very official, Miss Riddell," he said. "What enquiries are these?"

"The death of Harry Common."

He frowned. "That was a bad business, but I understood from the police it was an accident, or manslaughter at most."

"I'm sure it was," Pauline said. "Only I want to understand what he was doing in town and at that pub. His mother said he went there on business, but she didn't know what kind of business. I hoped you might."

"Oh, I see. I really can't help you, I'm afraid. He wasn't there on my business, if that's what you thought."

"I hoped you might know who Harry would do business with in Durham?" Pauline said. "Maybe someone from when the mine was operating or someone that Harry has bought materials from in the past?"

He shook his head. "Our suppliers were always more

Newcastle based, rather than Durham," he said, thoughtfully. "Durham isn't exactly an industrial sort of place."

"Can you tell me about Harry?" Pauline asked. "You seem to have had some respect for him, above the others, I mean."

"I did," Sir Robert said. "He was the kind of go-ahead man the north needs. Not just a nine-to-five kind of person, you know."

"I understand you'd given him work since the mine was closed."

"He set up in business making and repairing metalwork items and I've given him some commissions, yes," he said. "He repaired the main gates you drove through on your way up to the house today, for example."

"And you let him stay on at the cottage."

"The cottage has a workshop attached," he replied, "which made it an excellent base for Harry. So again, yes, I did."

"There's nothing you can think of to explain him being in Durham that night?"

"We weren't partners, Miss Riddell. Harry ran his own business and didn't need to include me in what he was doing. I imagine someone offered him work and they arranged to meet at that pub. Maybe it was convenient for both parties."

"Sadly, Harry's business was very informal, his mother says. There was no paperwork at all."

Sir Robert laughed. "Well, he wasn't yet one of the country's engineering giants. So long as he satisfied the tax man each April, he wouldn't need much paperwork."

"Do you know if someone did his taxes?" Pauline asked, sensing a possible lead.

"I don't, I'm sorry."

"Apart from his business energies, what was Harry like as a person?"

"An interesting fellow," Sir Robert said. "We had a lot in common."

"Such as?"

"A love of our history and a belief the north needs to manage its own affairs here and not through the dead hand of London, for example."

"You probably thought the Lindisfarne Gospels should be permanently on display here in the north, rather than just loaned back to us," Pauline asked.

"We did. We talked of that more than once since the visit was announced. It's outrageous when you think about it. That a northern national treasure could only be allowed to visit for a few days before being taken away again."

"There are many examples of such things," Pauline said. "What makes this one special?"

"Neither of us thought it was special," Sir Robert said. "These antiquities are rightly called national treasures, but they wouldn't be leaving the nation if they were on display where they were created. All those other treasures should be the same."

"Did you plan to go and see the Gospels book when it was here?"

"Oh, I saw it on the day set aside for we 'worthies'," Sir Robert said, with a smile. "Harry planned to go one evening. Maybe that was the evening."

Pauline shook her head. "The Gospels weren't on show that day and Harry would surely have heard that. The news was everywhere."

The door opened and a woman entered pushing a wheeled trolley with cups, teapot, and a small, tiered cake stand.

"Thank you, Betty," Sir Robert said, and waited while the server poured two cups. "We'll manage from here," he told her, with one of his brilliant smiles.

When Betty had left them, he said, "Again, Miss Riddell, if what you say is correct, I can't suggest anything new."

Pauline, who could never resist pastries, helped herself to a Bakewell Tart before asking, "Is it possible Harry's belief the Gospels should reside in the north might have led him to consider, shall we say, liberating them?"

Sir Robert laughed and shook his head. "Of the two of us, that would more likely be me."

Pauline smiled. "And did you? Consider liberating them, I mean?"

"I certainly fantasized about saving them for the north," he said. "But I didn't consider it, no. Like Harry, I think the world works best if you work within the rules." He paused, then asked, "You aren't saying the Gospels have been liberated, are you?"

Pauline shook her head, vehemently. Then realized maybe a bit too vehemently and toned it down before saying, "Not at all. I just wondered if that was the business that took Harry to Durham."

"I see, yes. He was casing the joint. Isn't that what they say on films when robbers are scouting out the ground?"

"Probably," Pauline said. "It would explain why he was in Durham when, as you said, his focus for his and your business was always Newcastle."

"Maybe he didn't hear the news about them being taken off display and only found out when he got to the cathedral," Sir Robert said. "Then decided to have a pie and a pint before traveling home."

"Maybe," Pauline said. "I hear you're a collector of antiquities, Sir Robert."

"I am and most of them to do with the north. If you're interested, I could show you after you've finished your tea."

"I'd like that," Pauline said. "I've never given our heritage much thought until this event, and I now see I should have taken more interest. In my school history, we touched on the Roman presence up here but not much else."

He nodded. "You'll find most of my collection is Roman. They were the most advanced of the people who lived here in the centuries before us. Apart from the brief flowering under the Anglian kings before the Vikings arrived and destroyed everything. Not too much collectible is to be found until the 1700s I'm afraid."

"Castles and forts are hard to collect," Pauline said, laughing.

"Exactly, though I have the remains of a small, unimportant castle in my grounds here so in a sense I've collected one."

"We found flint arrowheads on the moors, when I was a child," Pauline said. "I still have one somewhere. I keep it for luck."

"I thought I detected a northern accent under all that private school tone," Sir Robert said. "Yorkshire?"

"The North Riding to be precise," Pauline said. "The finest spot on God's green earth." Her heart skipped a beat and a sharp pain gripped her. Her silly lover's squabbles with Stephen about where they would live. She holding forth for the North Riding of Yorkshire and he holding out for Northumberland. She blinked to prevent the tears that she felt welling in her eyes.

"It is a lovely spot," he agreed, "but you'll have to

forgive me for saying it's only just pipped by County Durham and Weardale in particular."

Pauline smiled. "I'll forgive you because I must. Your hometown pride has clearly colored your vision and I can understand that. I've finished my tea, thank you. Can we view your collection?"

Sir Robert's collection of antiquities was extensive and as he'd said, overwhelmingly Roman. From Pauline's point of view, however, what was interesting were items from religious sites around the north.

In answer to her question, Sir Robert replied, "Most of these items were collected before the ruins were protected. When I was young, we played on many of the ruins, and no one thought anything of it."

"These are from Fountains Abbey?" Pauline asked, pointing at pieces of pottery in shallow wooden boxes, all neatly labeled.

"Yes, and over here, from Rievaulx Abbey," he replied, carrying on to the next case. "People down the centuries took the stones, lead, and glass to build their houses but no one had much use for the pieces of parchment or rotted shelves where books and parchments once stood."

"The Gospels would sit nicely among all these, don't you think?" Pauline asked.

"The Gospels are from five hundred years before these religious relics, Miss Riddell, and two to three hundred years after my Roman relics. They would be quite out-of-place in my small collection, as I'm sure you know."

Pauline felt herself flush. *A bit too obvious there, Pauline*, she thought.

"Naturally the book would have a properly arranged place," she said. "I simply meant it would fit into this corner of religious artifacts."

He laughed. "I suspect the Gospels would be outraged at being close to them. They were created by monks living an austere life in simple surroundings. The great abbeys lived when the church had grown very rich. The Lindisfarne Gospels, if a book could have an opinion, would not approve, I'm sure."

"You're probably right," Pauline said. "Though I suspect they would welcome a home where they were appreciated and not a museum where they were simply displayed. And as for the abbeys, I'd be on the side of the Gospels there too. I favor a simpler church as well, you see. The book, which I hope to see one evening this week, will speak to me better than any great abbey."

"I like both," Sir Robert said, nodding in response, "the majestic beauty of the great abbeys and the simpler beauty of the Gospels. They both show the best in us, and they should both be here where they were created. If they could be moved, you can be sure the abbey ruins would have been taken to London as well."

Pauline laughed. "I think that, if the Gospels go missing, I'll know where to look for them."

Smiling, he shook his head. "You and many others, Miss Riddell. I told everyone at the cocktail party during our private viewing of the Gospels I thought they should stay here in the north. I'm sure they will all remember if they go missing."

"Fortunately, they're well protected," Pauline said, "and unlikely to go missing."

He nodded. "Yes, fortunately, they are, or I'd be besieged here in my castle and this modern castle isn't meant for such things."

"Have you been approached by anyone wishing to sell the Gospels?"

"No," he said, smiling. "I would know they were stolen property. Do you think it likely someone might be trying to sell them, Miss Riddell?"

Pauline explained about the Catholic women activists, the poverty activists, and the northern nationalist activists. "The poverty activists, I'm sure would like cash," she said, when she'd finished explaining.

"I know the leaders of that protest," Sir Robert said. "The unions were always trying to enlist my mine workforce and the metalworkers were the most persistent of the lot. Their leader is an unpleasant man called Temperley."

"You said Harry was a metalworker, would he have known the union leaders?"

Sir Robert nodded. "He did. They wanted Harry to be the shop steward of the newly unionized metalworkers at the mine. It was a blatant bribe, to be frank. They knew if Harry joined, the others would to."

"And Harry wouldn't?"

"Harry understood our small pit could never pay union wages. Sadly, too many of the men didn't understand that and when the government nationalized all the mines, they finally got their way. Their happiness only lasted a very few years for it was as I'd always told them. The seam wasn't economical as a mass-producing pit. Ours was a small operation supplying the locals in the area around us."

"Harry's mum told me," Pauline said, nodding.

"The workers were offered work at bigger mines, and some left to take up those positions, but most were too old, or too set in their ways to leave and were made redundant. They were very bitter."

"Harry's mum said they were angry against Harry, even though he'd tried to warn them."

He laughed. "You'll find in life, Miss Riddell, that

people blame those who try to save them rather than those who do them harm. It's human nature, I'm afraid."

"Even though it makes no sense?"

He nodded. "I'm afraid so. Humans are strange creatures. If you save them today, they'll say you should have done it earlier, or better. They're rarely upset at the people you saved them from. I can't explain it."

"I'm not sure I can agree with you there, Sir Robert," Pauline said. "Maybe I just haven't yet had enough experience of people. Anyway, I've taken up a lot of your time. Is there anything you can think of that might help me that we haven't talked about?"

"Not at present but if I do, where shall I find you?"

Pauline, tearing another page from her notebook, gave him her phone number. He escorted her to the door, inviting her to visit again and spend more time studying his collection. She thanked him, and decided she would return because, for all his affability, he would be someone who would want the Lindisfarne Gospels in his grasp.

It was dark by the time she reached home and settled herself in a chair around the fire with the Bertrams. On her answering their question where she'd been, they immediately wanted to hear all she could tell them about Sir Robert Lauriston. Unknown to Pauline he might have been, but to local people he was a well-known and extremely popular figure in the district.

Pauline did her best to explain her visit and describe what she saw at his home. Finally they ran out of questions, and she was able to pick up her book.

Chapter Nine

POPPY'S ARTICLE

PAULINE HAD ONLY JUST BEGUN READING when the phone rang.

"I'll get it," Mr. Bertram said, rising ponderously from his armchair. "Who can it be at this time of night?"

He left the room and they heard him briefly acknowledge the caller. He returned to the room and said, "It's Poppy for you, Pauline."

Wishing she could pretend she wasn't there, Pauline left the room closing the door behind her and picked up the handset. "Poppy, how nice of you to call," Pauline said brightly, hoping her misgivings weren't apparent in her voice.

"Have the Gospels been stolen?" Poppy demanded. "Is that why Ramsay couldn't tell me about it?"

"Inspector Ramsay wanted me to speak to some women involved in an investigation he's on," Pauline said. "He thought a woman asking the questions may get more from the witnesses. That's all."

"But the Gospels are stolen," Poppy said. It wasn't even a question.

"The news on the radio said the conservator from London had examined them and they were back on display today," Pauline replied.

"I know what they want us to think," Poppy said. "But you can't kid a kidder. I'm in the business, Pauline. I smell a rat and I'm sure you know what I mean."

"I don't know anything of the sort, Poppy," Pauline said. "I only know what I heard on the radio."

"Suit yourself," Poppy said. "Oh, there are the time 'pips' and I have no more money. See my article tomorrow. It's your fault if it's wrong." Her voice was cut off as her phone time ran out.

If Pauline cursed this would have been the time to do it, but she didn't. She phoned Inspector Ramsay instead.

He listened in grim silence while she explained. When she'd finished, he said, "Your friend is going to be a problem."

"Which is why I phoned you. Is there nothing the police can do to stop the article going out?"

"If this was a national security affair, I'm sure we could. But we haven't yet descended into that kind of behavior over nothing more than an embarrassing crime," Ramsay replied. "I'll phone the Scotland Yard man and let him decide."

"I think she might implicate me in some way," Pauline said. "Even if it's just to say she talked to renowned sleuth Miss Riddell who told her she wasn't working on the case."

"Using the press is a double-edged sword, Miss Riddell," Ramsay said. "They can build you up and cut you down, whatever suits their purpose on the day."

"I haven't used the press at all, Inspector. You know very

well I've tried to restrain Poppy at every turn," Pauline protested, incensed he understood so little of what she'd felt these past weeks.

"Nevertheless, your fame rests on her words and your reputation does too. Beware of Greeks bearing gifts, isn't that what they say?"

"She threatened me, you know," Pauline said. "Not with violence. She said it was my fault if the article is wrong. I'm sure she'll present the story in a way that will make it my fault."

Ramsay was quiet for a moment. Long years of dealing with the crafty wordsmiths of the press had inured him to their behavior. Miss Riddell would learn the hard way she must say as little as possible to reporters. It was better she learned now when the stakes weren't high than on some future investigation where a wrong report could lead her into real danger.

"Your friend may have just been upset," he said at last, "and will think better of writing something that hurts you."

"I hope you're right," Pauline said. "Poppy was good to me when Stephen was killed. I'd hate us to become enemies."

She hung up the phone and returned to the sitting room where the Bertrams' anxious faces said they'd heard most of the conversation.

"Is everything all right, dear?" Mrs. Bertram asked.

"I hope so," Pauline replied guardedly. She would say nothing until she saw the article. After all, Poppy was their family, and they may take Poppy's part.

"Is Poppy writing another of her articles?" Mr. Bertram asked.

"Yes," Pauline said, "and it may be, um, controversial, you see."

"Oh dear," Mrs. Bertram said. "I hope she will be sensible."

"When was Poppy ever sensible?" her husband asked with a sardonic laugh.

"She's grown out of all that, I'm sure," Mrs. Bertram said. "She's been as good as gold where Pauline's been concerned."

Her husband shook his head and returned to his book. Pauline wished she knew what it was Poppy had grown out of and if it might have a bearing on the article she'd read in the morning papers.

Pauline hardly slept with wild thoughts about what Poppy might say and what it might do to Ramsay running through her mind. If she hinted Pauline was working with him on the investigation into the missing Lindisfarne Gospels, he might be out of a job.

Morning found her tired and unhappy. She hardly spoke at breakfast and the Bertrams seemed to understand for even Mrs. Bertram, usually the one to keep the conversation flowing, was silent.

As she left before the local paper was delivered, Pauline stopped on her way and bought the Newcastle and Morpeth papers. There was no article. Perhaps Ramsay had been right, and Poppy had thought better of it. She scanned the national papers on the shelves, but they were the early editions and couldn't have anything new from their Northern Correspondent, as Poppy now styled herself.

Her workday was equally as tense as her night had been because, Pauline realized, Poppy's article probably missed the morning editions and wouldn't appear until this evening. Her stomach in knots, Pauline went through the motions of work until even her usually unobservant boss was moved to ask if she was well.

"I'm sorry," Pauline said. "I'm worried about what my friend Poppy might say in her latest article." She'd explained to him more than once that Poppy was just a friend and not paid to promote the 'Miss Riddell's Detective Agency' he'd often joked about her starting.

"But she's always helped your cause," Dr. Enderby said. "Why would this be different?"

"She has taken it into her head the Lindisfarne Gospels have been stolen and I'm working on the case," Pauline said.

Enderby frowned. "Is she saying the announcement about them being held back for a day or two was false? And how could they be back on display if they've been stolen?"

Pauline explained Poppy's reasoning. He nodded and asked, "Is there any truth in it?"

"I know only what you know," Pauline said. "I couldn't convince Poppy of that."

"Well," Enderby said, "while I sympathize with your plight, I must have your full attention this afternoon. The meeting may well decide the outcome of our new contract and I need your notes to be an honest reflection of what is said. If you can't promise that I'll get someone else."

Pauline assured him of her attention and took a grip on her wooly mind. She wished she'd slept better. When lunch time came, she walked outside to let the wind and weather sharpen her wits.

On the drive home, she once again stopped at the newsagent's and examined several papers. Her heart sank. She'd hoped such an article would have been lost on a page in the middle of the paper. It wasn't. It wasn't *headline* news, but it was on the front page below the fold and each paper used a slightly different, but sensational headline intended to get a response from their readers.

Too many of them mentioned Miss Riddell for Pauline's comfort. She and Ramsay would have to work together to minimize the damage done to them. Others could fix the reputational damage to the cathedral, the British Museum, the local police, and those responsible for the Gospels' security. After her evening meal, she phoned Ramsay.

"I haven't seen the newspapers, Miss Riddell," Ramsay said, when she finally got through to him. "Your friend's article has appeared, I suspect?"

"It has," Pauline replied. "I don't like it and I'm sure you won't either. This will hit you first so we should think about what we're going to say."

"I need to read the articles before I can decide. Shall we say The Traveller's Rest in one hour?"

He was already waiting in the room set aside for those who wished to avoid the public bar when Pauline entered. He waved her over. "I bought your usual sherry, Miss Riddell," he said, by way of greeting.

Pauline handed over the four national newspapers and the local Morpeth Herald for him to read while she settled herself.

"You're right," he said, putting the first paper aside and starting to read the next. "I don't like it."

"I'm surprised there aren't reporters already outside the door," Pauline said. "There will be soon enough. She's blown this investigation completely apart."

He put down the paper and picked up the next before replying, "There'll be questions of the Government in the Parliament about the missing Gospels, I shouldn't wonder. They won't like that. They hate lying about inconsequential things where they might be found out."

"This is no time for your cynicism, Inspector," Pauline

said sharply. "Our lives are at stake here, not some nameless nobodies in government."

Ramsay laughed. "I'm sure the nameless nobodies are saying exactly the same thing but about you and me."

"And they have more power than we have," Pauline reminded him. "I'm too young to have my life ruined by this."

"You're beginning to sound like you finally understand the danger you put yourself in when you set out on your sleuthing pastime, Miss Riddell," Ramsay said. "Welcome to my world."

Pauline was about to say he was used to it, and she wasn't, then her usual calm returned. "Sorry," she said, smiling. "But it is a bit frightening. The thought that people far away in government might see me as the scapegoat for this."

Ramsay finished another paper and picked up the local one. "We must see that they can't link you to this irresponsible journalist's wild claim. The Lindisfarne Gospels aren't missing, and you are not looking into such a ridiculous notion."

"What am I looking into then?"

"Before I was transferred to the Artifacts Recovery Task Force," Ramsay said. "I was looking into a rash of thefts in Jesmond. Because many of the people who might have information were women, I asked if you could talk to them. Not police work, just an honest citizen showing interest in local affairs."

"That would explain why you invited my help before the Gospels were removed from display," Pauline agreed, "but what if any of the people I've talked to read the articles and decide to speak up?"

"You've spoken to them only about Harry Common, I hope?" Ramsay said.

Pauline nodded. "I have but again, why am I involved there?"

"Because my good friend Inspector Lawson of Durham Police is heading up that case. He and I talked about it, and I recommended that you talk to the women."

"I'm not sure I like this constant theme of I get to talk to the women, Inspector," Pauline said with a smile.

"People will accept it," Ramsay said. "Even those who would bristle at the suggestion will assume it's the sort of thing we'd do. It will reinforce their view of us, to be honest."

"Then it serves you right, too," Pauline said. "To be equally honest, that's exactly why I decided I wouldn't apply to join the police force."

Ramsay laughed. "Your opinion and theirs don't make me even a bit uncomfortable, Miss Riddell. Don't waste your effort trying."

"I suppose not," Pauline said. "One day, you'll realize how mistaken you were and then you'll be sorry."

"I think it more likely your experiences will show you I was right," he said. "It doesn't matter. That's the far future and we have a near future catastrophe to avert. If I can persuade my bosses of this version of events, will you support it?"

"Publicly?" Pauline could feel the blood draining from her face at the thought of being interviewed by hostile reporters or worse, radio and television interviewers.

"I'll suggest we issue a statement from you about what we've just said. That way you don't have to be put on the spot."

"Will your masters go for that?" Pauline asked.

"I'll point out to them you're a young woman without experience of public speaking and likely to stumble over your lines if you're challenged. I think they'll see the wisdom of keeping you off the frontline."

"Here's to that," Pauline said, lifting her glass and downing her sherry in one gulp. This case was curing her of any future involvement in crime.

Chapter Ten

RAMSAY'S DAY

AS HE ENTERED the Durham police headquarters building the following morning, Ramsay wasn't surprised to find two of the London detective sergeants waiting to escort him to the Task Force leader. He was shown into a paneled office, much grander than that usually assigned even to Chief Inspectors. He decided it was possibly the Chief Constable of Durham's office.

The commander told his two escorts to leave before throwing the pile of newspapers he was holding onto the desk that was between them.

"What the hell is this?" the man demanded, his southern accent grating on Ramsay's ears.

"It's an irresponsible young journalist making a name for herself by causing trouble," Ramsay replied evenly.

"And who exactly is this Miss Riddell you work with?"

"You likely wouldn't have heard of the cases," Ramsay said. "She's a young woman who was instrumental in bringing some murderers to justice," Ramsay said.

"Up here it's open house on criminal investigation, is it?"

The man was clearly working himself up into a rage, which didn't bode well for Ramsay's future on the team or maybe even in the force, Ramsay thought. "It isn't. Miss Riddell was involved because she knew the people," Ramsay said, not entirely truthfully. "And her insights brought the cases to a close quicker than we who were investigating from the outside could have done, as it were."

"These articles say she's working with you on the missing Gospels," his boss yelled. "No one is supposed to know they're missing, you idiot."

The London man had reached a good state of fury now. His face was practically purple, and spittle flew from his lips as he yelled. Ramsay had some sympathy for the man. The politicians would pounce on him first and he'd likely be their first sacrificial victim. Ramsay's sympathy wasn't, however, very strong. The man was a tyrant to his subordinates and generally unpleasant to everyone else.

"The reporter is taking a stab in the dark," Ramsay said. "She knew Miss Riddell was questioning some people on my behalf, heard the Gospels were taken off display, and added the two things together to make a false story that looks just good enough to hold water, the way these muckrakers usually do."

"So, you don't have this woman working on my case?"

"How could I when no one knows the Gospels are missing?" Ramsay replied. The fact he was doing what he'd just accused journalists of doing didn't concern him at all.

"Then why does this woman think she is working on the case?"

"Like I said, sir. She knows I asked Miss Riddell to make some enquiries for me just before I joined this team. The case had a lot of female witnesses and I felt Miss Riddell may have more success than a man might. The journalist used this as evidence to back up her wild claim the Gospels had been stolen."

His boss eyed him suspiciously. "Nevertheless, this has put us all in a bind. We'll have half our people fending off the press and officialdom instead of focusing on the job."

Ramsay nodded. "I realize that, sir."

"Can you get your Miss Riddell to make a statement explicitly rejecting this article? I say article because it really is just one that's been re-written for a variety of audiences."

"It will have to be something she believes in," Ramsay said. "She's not someone who can tell lies in public."

"Then she has no business actively going out and about in public," his boss growled. "Bring her in and we'll work on her."

"I think that might make everyone believe the story is true," Ramsay said. "Much better we craft a statement for her to read and approve and we release it to the press."

"The press won't accept that. They'll hound her wherever she goes."

"She'll understand she mustn't say anything beyond the statement, and she must not, under any circumstances, speak to her reporter friend again."

His boss considered. "Very well. Get the media man on it and you run it by me before it goes to her, right?"

"Yes, sir," Ramsay said, relieved. Now he and the police media officer had only to write the story he'd prepared with Miss Riddell using words his bosses could accept, too. That was the trouble with honest people like Miss Riddell, he thought, they never could quite understand honesty isn't always the best policy.

By nine that morning, Ramsay and their press officer

had words Ramsay felt Pauline could live with. With these in hand, Ramsay found a small office, away from the team. With the press man, they phoned Pauline at work.

She wasn't surprised when he told her why he was phoning and listened patiently as he read the statement to her. As he spoke, she wrote the words in shorthand.

"I know time is of the essence here, Inspector," she told him. "But I need a few minutes to read this through and make myself comfortable with it. We both know that it isn't what the witness stand oath would call 'the whole truth' and I want to be sure I can live with myself after saying this."

He gave her the phone number and hung up. Pauline read the statement through slowly, considering each word, each phrase, and the whole paragraph taken together. She admired the way it was framed and how it didn't say anything that wasn't true. It put Poppy on the spot for she had no actual proof of anything she'd written, her article had been all 'rumors say'.

It also gave Pauline some measure of satisfaction that the statement was written in the same duplicitous wording Poppy's article had used so in a sense it served Poppy right. But it was an uncomfortable feeling; she was drawing a line between herself and her friend that would never be quite erased. Had Poppy felt this way when she'd written her article? If she had, she'd submitted it knowing what it would do to Pauline and Ramsay.

Pauline phoned Ramsay back and confirmed she could accept the statement and would make no changes.

"You'll be harassed by reporters for a time," Ramsay said. "You mustn't deviate from this at any time. You realize that?"

"I do," Pauline said, grimly. "My answer will be 'I've

nothing to add to my statement.' I'm sure they'll eventually lose interest."

"We must hope so," Ramsay said. "Don't speak to your friend Poppy again until after this is over."

"At this moment, I'm not sure I want to speak to her ever again," Pauline said emphatically.

Ramsay laughed. "Keep feeling that way until the case is closed. Then you can mend fences."

All afternoon, Pauline waited in trepidation expecting the phone to ring and Ramsay to say their path forward had not been accepted. By mid-afternoon, she was feeling so ill she was ready to call him, when the phone rang. She grabbed the handset and had demanded 'Yes?' before she realized it may not be Ramsay on the phone and that was no way to answer calls to her boss's office.

"Yes, Miss Riddell," Ramsay said. "The statement has been issued along with an official denial that the Gospels are missing. Now you must keep your nerve when they come for you."

Pauline sighed with relief. She'd known how upset she was but not how her whole being felt it was holding its breath.

"You can count on me, Inspector. This is my life at stake here, too."

He laughed. "I'm not sure our actual lives are at stake, Miss Riddell, though I know how you feel. Avoid any investigating while the reporters are about, won't you?"

"I'll confine myself to the Harry Common's and the Jesmond robberies' stories, you can be sure." She was suddenly aware that he too may have been shunted aside, and asked, "What will you be doing?"

"I'm still concentrating on the bank robbery, which has

a Newcastle connection," he replied. "We both live to fight another day, you see."

After the evening meal, Pauline and the Bertrams settled down in the living room. Mr. Bertram and Pauline reading their books and Mrs. Bertram with her knitting. The radio played relaxing music and a glowing coal fire warmed them. A perfect evening. Until the phone rang.

"Will that be for you, dear?" Mrs. Bertram asked.

"I hope not," Pauline replied. "If it is, please say I'm not yet home from work."

"Even if it's Inspector Ramsay?" Mrs. Bertram asked as she headed out to the hall where the telephone was kept.

"I'll only speak with him," Pauline said. "I imagine it's reporters and I haven't the strength to face them right now."

Pauline listened intently as Mrs. Bertram picked up the handset. "Oh. Hello, Poppy," she said, glancing back into the living room to see if Pauline was taking notice.

Pauline shook her head angrily. Of all the reporters she didn't want to talk to, Poppy was the one she didn't want to talk to the most.

Mrs. Bertram made her excuses and assured Poppy she'd tell Pauline the moment she got in. She hung up the phone and returned to her seat.

"Poppy wants to talk to you urgently," she said, picking up her knitting.

"I'm sure she does," Pauline said. "I, however, don't want to speak to her until I'm calm enough to do it without yelling at her."

"It said in the paper the government issued a statement today," Mr. Bertram said.

"And you can imagine how pleased they will be about

that," Pauline said. "I'm angry because I had to make a statement too, and I'm not nearly as important as they are."

"I saw it in the evening paper," Mrs. Bertram said. "It sounded most unlike you."

"That's because it wasn't me, at least not the final words. They were written by the police press officer in words suitable for the press. They aren't happy either."

"Poppy's nonsense hasn't hurt your friend Inspector Ramsay, has it?" Mr. Bertram asked.

"He and I will be under terrible suspicion going forward," Pauline said, "but he thinks we'll come out of it intact. At least, he says we won't lose our lives over it." She smiled to show it was a joke. Though she now finally realized that he and she could have lost their lives on her very first case if things had gone differently. It made his joke this time not as re-assuring as she'd at first thought.

"She was always headstrong and willful," Mr. Bertram said seriously. "I do hope the results of all this will teach her a lesson she won't forget."

"You never approved of Poppy, dear," Mrs. Bertram said. "I'm sure she meant no harm. She's a good girl really."

Mr. Bertram returned to his book without further comment. Pauline thought he would have liked to disagree with his wife on how good a girl Poppy was but chose not to. Once again, she'd gained an insight into Poppy that had been hidden before. Stephen had liked her, and his recommendation had been enough for Pauline.

"I hope this means you won't be doing any more horrible investigations for Inspector Ramsay," Mrs. Bertram said. "He's a nice man but he shouldn't involve a young woman like you in the criminal world."

Pauline didn't reply. Like Mr. Bertram, she took shelter in her book.

There was silence for a few minutes, broken only by the click-click of the knitting needles. Then Mrs. Bertram said, "You won't leave it too long before you talk to Poppy, will you dear? I'm sure neither of you will be best served by an unpleasant break."

"I'll phone her tomorrow," Pauline said. "I just need to clear my head of angry thoughts and clear my mouth of the unpleasant taste that statement has left."

"Oh, good. Poppy probably realizes she made an awful mistake…" she paused to glare at her husband who'd given a disbelieving snort, before ending, "and wants to apologize."

In order to avoid replying, Pauline went out to the hall, opened the telephone book, and found the number for the leader of the religious protesters.

She hesitated a moment. She'd told Ramsay she'd avoid the Gospels case for a time. Then, with a firm action, spun the telephone dial to the woman's number. The woman seemed pleasantly surprised at having a local celebrity call her and agreed to Pauline's suggestion to meet and talk.

"Thank you, Mrs. Thompson," Pauline said. "I'll see you tomorrow evening." She hung up the phone and returned to the sitting room.

"Did you phone Poppy?" Mrs. Bertram asked.

Pauline shook her head. "No. I phoned a woman who is protesting against the Church of England."

Mrs. Bertram was shocked. "Really, dear? How awful. I hope you gave her a piece of your mind."

"I might," Pauline said, smiling. "I'm going straight to her home tomorrow after work. I'll be back late."

Chapter Eleven

PAULINE BEGINS HER INVESTIGATION

PAULINE RANG the doorbell on a nicely kept Victorian house just across the river from Durham cathedral and waited for Theresa Thompson to open the door. When she did, Pauline was mildly surprised. She'd half expected something wilder in her appearance. What she saw was a slim, middle-aged woman with a pleasant face and a warm smile.

"Miss Riddell?" the woman asked.

"That's me," Pauline replied. "Are you Mrs. Thompson?"

"Yes, but call me Theresa," the woman replied. "Now, do come in. It's a cold night to stand at the door."

"Only if you'll call me Pauline," Pauline said, stepping inside.

Pauline followed her into a well-furnished sitting room, rather overly furnished in Pauline's opinion for she didn't care for what people called knick-knacks. They were everywhere, with the mantelpiece above the fireplace particularly crowded with small figurines displaying the names of many different towns in Britain and France, many with a religious theme.

Mrs. Thompson gestured her to take a seat and asked if she'd like tea. Pauline took the offered seat on the couch but declined the tea.

"Have you been to all these places in France?" Pauline asked, pointing to the figurines.

"Oh, yes," Mrs. Thompson said, seeing where Pauline was looking. "After the war, I made it my point to visit the continent. After all, so much had been closed to us for so long."

"You're so fortunate," Pauline said. "I haven't yet saved enough money to visit Scotland, never mind the continent." She laughed.

"I am fortunate, of course," Mrs. Thompson said, but her face was grave. "But it was at too high a price. Much of my travel has been on my husband's life insurance payout."

Pauline mentally cursed herself for not suspecting. After all, it was a common enough tale nowadays. "I'm sorry to hear that. As you say, too high a price."

Mrs. Thompson nodded. "He said I was lucky. If he'd been killed outright in the war, I'd have got nothing more than a widow's pension. As it was, the treatment he received in the Japanese camps didn't kill him right away, just ensured he lingered on into peacetime to die of natural causes."

"Your faith must help," Pauline said.

"It does," Mrs. Thompson replied, "though it also makes me doubt. I understand you go to church so you might understand."

Better than you can know, Pauline thought. "Yes, I do see that. Now, as I told you on the phone, Inspector Ramsay asked me to help with an investigation that isn't really police work."

"Your adventures these past months," Mrs. Thompson said, smiling, "have made you a minor celebrity. Inspector Ramsay, too."

Pauline laughed. "He wouldn't thank you for saying that. He and his superiors don't often see eye-to-eye and knowing he was becoming famous above his station would make things worse."

"Bosses are like that, aren't they?"

"I'm sure many are," Pauline said, "though I have to put in a good word for my own boss who has always been supportive."

"Mine doesn't like me trying, in my own time, to have the great wrong done to our church in the Reformation put right. He thinks it will get him involved."

"Don't you work for the church?"

Mrs. Thompson shook her head. "Even if I did, they'd do all they could to shut me up, you can be sure. My parish priest is always being asked to stop me."

Pauline laughed. "Your church doesn't want to re-open a four-hundred-fifty-year-old quarrel, I suppose."

"It doesn't," Theresa said, "and in general I agree with them. There's no sense in arguing over Fountains Abbey or Tintern Abbey; they're ruins now. But the cathedrals the Anglican Church is using today, and many of the churches it uses, were built nearly a thousand years ago by the Catholic Church and it's time they were handed back. They were taken by force, and we were never compensated."

"And that's true of the Lindisfarne Gospels?"

Theresa smiled mischievously. "Not exactly," she said, "but even they're more ours than the British Museum's, and their coming here is a great opportunity to raise the issue to a wider public."

"Everybody seems to see the arrival of the Gospels as a way to raise issues to a wider public."

Theresa nodded. "We noticed. Communists want to use them to talk about poverty and depressed regions. That surprised us, I can tell you. I thought, as atheists, they wouldn't even know what the Gospels were."

Pauline smiled. "They know they're valuable to important people and that's enough to get them excited. And who knew we had Northern England separatists?"

Theresa nodded. "I'd never even heard of such a thing but there they were, demanding all Northumbria's treasure returned to Northumbria and the region's borders aligned along that of the Seventh Century Anglican kingdom. How the Scots and their Nationalists would like that, I can't imagine. Northumbria included most of what is now southeastern Scotland."

"You must have heard them talking, even spoken to some of them," Pauline said. "Did you hear anyone mention a man called Harry Common?"

"I read about his death in the paper," Theresa said. "I can't believe anyone in any of the protest groups had anything to do with it. The nationalists are just dreamers, and the trades unionists, though rough-looking men, struck me as being better at organizing industrial unrest rather than killing people."

"The death may have been an accident," Pauline said. "It seems Mr. Common had a rare disease that made his bones brittle."

"Then it could have been any of the men," Theresa said.

"Not your small group?"

Theresa laughed. "We might wield a savage handbag, but I fear we couldn't hit even a damaged man hard enough to kill him."

"Have you heard of any of the groups talking about stealing the Gospels?" Pauline asked. "You'll have seen the articles I'm sure and the statements regarding the notion they'd been stolen. I wondered where the reporter might have heard such talk?"

"Oh," Theresa said. "That's easy. On the morning they announced the Gospels wouldn't be on show that day, there were lots of people joking they'd been stolen."

"Among your group?" Pauline asked. "Surely, you'd be happy to have them in your possession?"

"Good gracious, no," Theresa said. "What would we do with the Gospels? Without a place to show them, a place for the faithful to pilgrimage to, they'd be no use. We need the buildings, churches and cathedrals first, the relics after."

"Do you really imagine that one day, the Anglican Church will say 'You're right. None of this belongs to us. Take it all back?'"

"Stranger things have happened," Theresa said. "Saul on the road to Damascus, for example."

"But the Anglican congregation might not accept their leader's decision."

"There's always the possibility of the Anglican Church willingly returning to the bosom of the mother faith," Theresa said. "Our activism may seem eccentric to you, Miss Riddell, but we will chip away at the problem and one day a solution will be found."

Pauline smiled. "I didn't really come here this evening to discuss your cause," she said. "I came to ask what you saw, what you noticed while you were protesting. There might be a link between Harry Common and the protests, you see.

He was a member of the Metalworkers Union, and their leader is the man leading the poverty protesters. What do you remember about that time?"

"Nothing that would help you, Miss Riddell," Theresa said, seriously. "Truly, nothing seemed in any way out of the ordinary."

"You didn't see this man?" she handed over the photo of Harry she'd borrowed from Mrs. Common.

Theresa studied it and shook her head. "I don't think I've ever seen this man," she said. "Though, to be fair, he looks very ordinary, and he wouldn't stand out in a crowd."

"Sadly, you're right," Pauline said. "Common by name and common in appearance and I don't mean that in any unkind way. He's a perfectly pleasant looking man you can see on any street in the land on any day of the year. I fear no one will remember him being at the cathedral, even if he was."

"Someone might," Theresa said. "Come by one evening and ask."

"I'm coming to see the Gospels one evening this week after work," Pauline said. "I'll show everyone the photo then. I only hope they won't be taken off show again before I see them. Had you seen it before? In the British Museum?"

"Oh no. I wouldn't travel all the way down there for anything," Theresa replied. "London is such a sinful place. I shouldn't feel safe."

Pauline laughed. "You sound like my friend Inspector Ramsay," she said. "He thinks London the root of all evil in this country."

"Is he Catholic?"

Pauline shook her head, smiling. "He's a lapsed Presbyterian but I don't think views about big cities necessarily align with our religious persuasions."

"It's true. There are many things we can all agree on. Now, what else can I tell you?"

"How is your protest going? Are you winning any converts?"

Theresa shook her head. "One never knows, really."

"What about the men who shift the book to and from the cathedral? Do you try to convert them?"

Theresa laughed. "They're a grim bunch. They pretend we aren't there."

"Do you speak to them?"

"No. Our signs say all we needed to say."

"What does yours say?" Pauline asked, intrigued.

"*Return What Was Stolen*," Theresa said. "It's hard to make a cogent argument on a small sign."

"Aren't you concerned people will think you're, well, a bit dotty? Asking for things taken centuries ago?"

"The Spanish waited more than seven centuries to recover their land and their religion," Theresa said. "I've no doubt that many Spanish people along the way were considered *dotty* by their fellow sufferers but they prevailed in the end. We will too, though perhaps not in my lifetime."

"Did you consider protesting at the Lowther Bank?"

Theresa looked momentarily unsettled but replied, "No. The bank has no role in this. Besides, I bank there, and the manager is a friend of mine. Or to be precise, he was a friend of my husband's when we were all much younger and he has been a friend to me since my husband died."

"You didn't sense the other protesters were more than just protesting?"

"There were some words between the nationalists and

the poverty people, who all seemed to be from a trade union, I gather."

"Hard words?"

Theresa frowned. "I find it hard to be sure with working men," she said. "Their accents are so thick and their voices so harsh, I never know if they're about to start fighting or about to link arms and unite against the world."

"Guess," Pauline said.

"I think they were close to fighting," Theresa said. "The union men seemed anti-nationalism and the northern nationalists seemed anti-communism. That's what I got from their words, but as I say, I could have it all wrong. They could have been joking. The way men do."

"Did they appear to watch the arrival and removal closely?"

Theresa laughed. "They weren't there in the morning. Still in bed, I'd say. Most of the northern nationalists came after three so I imagine they'd been to work. The union men were there from lunch time, so I doubt they work at all."

"They may work in the local union headquarters and aren't bound to a clock," Pauline said. Why she felt she needed to defend them, she didn't know. It just seemed fair.

"There really is nothing useful I can tell you, Miss Riddell. I'm sorry."

"You've given me a good insight into the day's events and that in itself is a help," Pauline said. "Thank you."

Outside, it was already dark with a thin mizzling rain falling, creating haloes around the streetlamps. As she walked quickly back to her car, Pauline wondered about Theresa Thompson. While her cause seemed ludicrous, Theresa herself seemed level-headed and capable. Pauline would get Inspector Ramsay to dig up some background.

Meanwhile, she needed to find the leader of the northern separatists whose name hadn't appeared in the phone book, and she had no idea where to start. First, however, she needed to speak to Poppy. Despite Inspector Ramsay's advice, Mrs. Bertram was right. She mustn't leave it too long or Poppy's mood might swing further and further in the direction of harming Pauline.

There was no point trying to phone Poppy. She wouldn't be in the office at this time of night, and she hadn't a phone in her flat. Pauline drove straight north, through Newcastle and up the Great North Road to Morpeth. When Pauline arrived, she found Poppy wasn't in her flat. The first place Pauline could think of to try was the newspaper offices, so she walked there.

She saw Poppy through the window and signaled her to come out, which she did.

"I haven't long," Poppy said. "We're working on a story for tomorrow morning's paper."

"I hope it isn't more about me and the Lindisfarne Gospels," Pauline said.

"It is, actually," Poppy said off-handedly while lighting a cigarette.

"Then don't, Poppy," Pauline said. "What you said in the last one wasn't true, and it has done terrible harm."

"I didn't say it was true," Poppy said, blowing out a cloud of smoke. "I said it was rumored and that you had denied it. I don't see why you're so upset."

"You know why I'm upset," Pauline said, smothering the urge to slap her friend. "The words said that – and everything else in the article said the opposite."

"I can't help how you read it," Poppy said. "What I said was basically true. There are rumors about the Gospels, and you did deny it. And I phoned you just yesterday for your side of the story. You didn't call back."

"Is that what you're writing now?" Pauline demanded. "More dangerous nonsense?"

"Not exactly," Poppy said, grinning. "I've never caused questions in Parliament before, and my editors want more. My struggle is to make the story deniable and believable. That isn't easy, you know." She was clearly enjoying this encounter.

Pauline was suddenly filled with loathing for this woman she'd thought of as a friend. A memory sprung into her head. Those first meetings when she'd suspected Poppy was using her for her own ends and how, over time, she, Pauline, had lowered her guard. She'd been right then. Poppy may have been building Miss Riddell's career, but that was incidental to building Poppy's Northern Correspondent career.

"You never liked me, did you?" Pauline said, unable to hold back.

Poppy shrugged. "You're the one who went off with the old policemen leaving your 'almost' family out in the cold."

"He explained that and promised you the scoop," Pauline cried. "What more could we have done?"

"Trusted me to help," Poppy said angrily.

"Like you're helping now?"

"That time has passed," Poppy said, dropping her cigarette end on the pavement and crushing it in a particularly meaningful way. "I have to get back inside." She turned and walked back to the office, slamming the door behind her.

Pauline returned to the Bertrams', almost in shock. She felt numb, unable to comprehend the suppressed rage she'd just witnessed – and she herself felt. What could she tell the Bertrams? She decided not to tell them anything. Instead, she stopped at a telephone box at the end of the street where the Bertrams lived and phoned Inspector Ramsay. He needed to know another article was on its way and it sounded as if it might be as damaging as the first had been.

Ramsay listened as Pauline described her encounter with Poppy. Then said seriously, "Miss Riddell, I thought you weren't going to speak to Poppy ever again? We'd agreed not to give her more ammunition."

Pauline blushed. "I thought it best to speak to her, try and make her see sense."

Ramsay shook his head in despair. "Well, at least this time the government ministers are aware of Poppy and her crusade. They will be less concerned now we have statements out denying everything."

"I'm concerned she may have dug up something new," Pauline said, relieved he wasn't going to continue being censorious. "She was awfully triumphant about her new article."

"She didn't give you any hint as to what it might be?"

"No and I wouldn't have given her the satisfaction of refusing to tell me if I had asked," Pauline replied.

"But she thinks it will be devastating?"

"She flat-out said her editors were impressed she'd managed to have questions asked in Parliament of the government and she was clearly aiming to repeat that feat."

"Governments have ways of silencing questions they don't want asked," Ramsay said. "She'll find it hard to catch them out twice."

"I have a question, Inspector," Pauline said. "Can you tell me where I can find the leader of the northern nationalist protesters?"

"Aye, if you go to the cathedral tomorrow night, they'll likely be there again," Ramsay said.

"Still, I'd like a name to know who to talk to."

"It's in the files. I'll phone from the office in the morning," Ramsay said.

"Thank you, Inspector. I need to stop myself fretting, you see. Poppy's article will keep me up all night if I can't find an alternative to think about."

"There's no sense in us guessing or worrying about that, Miss Riddell. We can only await publication and counter it then. Get a good night's sleep. You need to be on your best performance tomorrow."

Pauline hung up the phone and stood staring from the phone box into the night. Everything about her surroundings was familiar – the street, the houses, the streetlamps – yet she felt the world was shifting all around her. She felt dizzy, nauseous even, and this was before she ever knew what the article said. More than anything, it was the look on Poppy's face as she'd turned away from Pauline to go back to the office; her expression was triumphant but it was worse than that, it was almost mad.

Chapter Twelve

'NATIONALISTS'

GETTING to work was no problem for Pauline; reporters weren't early birds. She knew however, after work she may have to run a gauntlet of them at the factory gates or at the Bertram's house.

"It seems your friend is making waves again," Dr. Enderby said, as he returned from lunch to find Pauline at her desk nibbling unhappily on a currant slice.

"Did you see the Morpeth Herald?" Pauline asked.

"It was on the radio during lunch time," her boss said. "It made the Guardian this morning. You might want to leave early today to escape the city reporters."

"Thank you," Pauline said, her stomach sinking. "I think that would be wise too."

He shook his head, his expression solemn. "It can't go on, Pauline," he said. "You know that, don't you?"

Pauline nodded. "The weeks of this past year went by so fast, everything was a whirl," she said. "I never noticed how the world was creeping up on me. I have tried to keep it outside work."

"I know," Enderby said. "Only once again, it's creeping inside."

"It seemed harmless when Inspector Ramsay asked me to speak to some women because he feels the police need women officers and they'd respond better to me," Pauline said. "Then Poppy took it as an affront she couldn't be involved and began this," she struggled for words, "*campaign* against us both."

"I can understand why the Inspector wouldn't want the press involved," he said. "You clearly didn't know your friend well enough to find the right reasons for excluding her."

"All I see is the Inspector was right to exclude her," Pauline said. "If she'd approached any of the witnesses in this manner, they'd never have trusted anyone again as long as they lived."

"Well, think about your future, Pauline," Enderby said. "We can't have gangs of reporters around our factory gates every day waiting to interview you. It will upset people."

"I'm already thinking about it," Pauline said. "And I'll make up the time, you can be sure." And she *was* thinking of the future, only it was her future meeting with the protesters the moment she left work.

The afternoon was cold but dry, which Pauline was thankful for. It meant her quarry would likely be there. He wasn't hard to find. A burly man with unfashionably bushy red hair and the sort of complexion that one associated with drinkers.

"Mr. Batey?" Pauline asked as she approached him. "May I have a word?" Inspector Ramsay had been good as his word and phoned her the man's name.

"Are you press?" He asked gruffly.

"I'm afraid not. Just someone hoping to learn more

about a man named Harry Common and how that might tie into the people protesting the Gospels."

"Why?" he asked.

Pauline recited the explanation she'd practiced. "I'm trying to set Harry's mother's mind at rest, you see. She doesn't understand what he was doing in Durham or why he would be fighting with anyone. Did any of you, for instance, arrange to meet Harry Common the night he died?"

"No. First I heard of him was his death reported in the paper," Batey replied.

"I wondered, you see, if he was somehow involved in why the Gospels were suddenly removed from public viewing."

"You're asking the wrong people," he said. "Try the bishop and his pals. They'll know why they removed the Gospels. It seemed like they thought the book was too good for us plebs to see."

"Do you really think they were hiding the book from us all?" Pauline asked. "I admit I was disappointed. I was to see them soon with our church group. I'm relieved now they're back on display."

"Oh, you church lot will see them, I'll warrant," he said. "It's just us ordinary folk who might spoil it with our breath."

"Churchgoers are ordinary folk too," Pauline said, gently. "I presume you haven't yet seen the book. Didn't you and the others go in on the first day?"

"Nay. It's only an old book from a foreign religion. It's no interest to me," he said. Then as if realizing he hadn't properly explained his protest, continued, "What's important is that book was made here by our ancestors, and we should have it here where we can see it when we want."

"I do see your point," Pauline said. "You believed the authorities were holding back the book for a different reason than the one given. Did anything strike you as odd that night when it was being transferred from the cathedral to the police van? Anything that might explain why it was removed from view?"

"How do mean, like?"

"Did anyone say something that might indicate they were about to do something to it, damage or steal it maybe?"

"Nay. Thon women over there," he waved in the direction of a small group of women carrying signs, "wanted it, but they would do nothing," he said. "And the commies over there," he waved at the larger group who appeared to be working men, "want the government to sell it. They don't want it for themselves, being atheists, like."

Pauline frowned. "What about your group? Wouldn't you like to have it and keep it safe until you have a free Northumbria?"

"It's more use to us in the hands of the authorities," he said, shaking his head. "That way we always have an object to focus our fight."

"You say the women wouldn't have taken it," Pauline said. "Is that because they're just women or do you have some other reason for believing them innocent?"

He frowned. "They're all about praying, and chanting, and hoping, and having faith, and, well, you get the idea. No demands for their rights, just the usual religious hoping. That's why." He snorted. "If we'd all behaved like that down the centuries, we'd still be in the Dark Ages."

"True," Pauline said. "So, nothing in all this time has struck you as a pointer to why they were removed from view?"

"There's no mystery," he said. "Just the usual higher-ups' jealousy of the lower orders getting more than we should."

"You see," Pauline said, "I think the authorities may have placed it in safekeeping because they were afraid of it being stolen. Your group and the other two might have scared them."

He laughed. "Anything's possible. Certainly, the gang over there," he pointed again to the poverty protesters, "would frighten anyone. Real hard cases, some of them. Union thugs, for the most part."

Pauline nodded. "They do look more threatening than you and the Catholic ladies. To return to my earlier question, didn't the name Harry Common mean anything to you?"

He shook his head. "As I said, only as the man who died in that pub fight the other night. Why?"

"I just wondered," Pauline said. "There's so much passion been raised by the Gospels' visit; I can't believe it isn't connected. He died just the day after they were removed from view, for instance."

"Sorry, can't help you there," Batey said, nodding dismissal.

Pauline looked across the cathedral's lawn with its shadowy grave markers to where the antipoverty protesters were being kept from the nationalist group by the lone policeman assigned to keep the peace. There was nothing for it. She had to go and talk to them as well. She could only hope none of them worked in the same factory she did and recognized or knew of her.

Chapter Thirteen

'COMMUNISTS'

THE RIVAL GROUP of protesters were, as Batey had described, a tougher looking bunch of men. Whereas the nationalists were burly and bearded wearing hiking clothes to keep out the cold, the antipoverty men wore jackets and ties of the sort working class men donned when in public. Their faces and expressions were hard, their frames lean and wiry from physical work. Pauline guessed their disagreement with the nationalist group was as much about the social gulf between office and shop floor as it was political.

"Mr. Temperley, I presume," Pauline said, approaching the man who appeared to be their leader and whose name Ramsay had given to her. He wasn't the name highlighted in the newspaper articles she'd read, which meant, in her mind, he was not their public face. Someone more sympathetic was.

"You another reporter?" the man asked.

"No, I'm an interested investigator looking into the

death of Harry Common and, incidentally, the rumor about the disappearance of the Gospels that keeps appearing in the papers. I think the two things might be related, you see."

"Then you're asking the wrong folks, lass," he said. "Folks like us don't even get to see stuff like that. It's snatched away before we can spoil it. That's what they said on the news, anyhow."

Pauline kept her tone neutral, though she was angered by this stretching the official story describing why the book was removed from view into evidence of the class struggle. "They said the conservators were concerned about the damp and how it might affect the ancient parchment."

He snorted. "The crowds and their damp breath are how the reporters described it."

"I didn't hear that," Pauline replied. "That was badly phrased, I'm sure. Anyway, the Gospels are back on display so they can't be too concerned about our damp breath, can they?" She looked to him for some glimmer of good will.

"Aye, they're back," he said tersely.

Pauline tried again. "But I have a different view of this. I think the authorities got wind of a plot to steal the Gospels and secured them until they were confident that wasn't the case."

"Aye," he replied. "Ought is possible with them folk."

"So, I was wondering if during your protests here, you'd heard anything that might support my theory?"

Temperley's expression became suspicious instantly. "Look, who are you?"

"Pauline Riddell. You might have seen my name in the papers recently."

"Oh, aye. I've seen your name all right. You're that nosy parker what identified some murderers."

"I like to see justice done," Pauline said.

"Well, if there's any justice in this world, it can't be seen around here," he said.

"Wouldn't it be a small piece of justice if I uncover the truth around this suspicious death and the book's temporary disappearance? Though really that's solved, now it's back on display."

He nodded slowly. "Is it back on display? I wouldn't be so sure about that. And about that fella that died, I can't help at all. I hardly knew him."

"Then you didn't arrange to meet with him the night he died?"

"Why would I?"

"I thought he might have been here to meet someone," Pauline said.

"Well, it weren't me," Temperley replied. "But if I can help get the real book back where it can be seen and sold, with the proceeds going to the people, I'll help."

Pauline frowned. "You think it's a copy on show?

"Course I do," he said. "So does anyone with a brain. Even the papers think so. Don't you read the papers?"

"Well," Pauline said, "if you're right and I can help find the real Gospels, I will. I can't promise to help sell it, but I can try to get it back where the people can claim it."

"You asked if I heard anything to suggest a theft," he said. "I didn't. The Catholic ladies are barmy enough to try to steal it, but unless it can be prayed out of the hands of the guards, they wouldn't have a clue. Yon fellows now," he pointed to the nationalists across the lawn, "they're different. They may look like clueless bearded folk singers but they're not all that way. Some of them are ex-army and know their way around devious plotting. They could."

"Did you hear anything that suggested they would?"

"Not as such," he admitted, "but they wanted that book for their own mad cause and fanatics are always dangerous."

"You said you knew Harry Common a little?" Pauline asked, pleased to see his expression change and a noticeably shiftier look to his eyes.

"A bit," he said.

"As an acquaintance?"

He shook his head. "He joined our union when the mine he worked at was nationalized, had to, like. I met him at the meetings, that's all. A canny lad. I was sorry to hear what happened to him."

"What union is that?"

"Metalworkers," he said. "Around here, we're one of the biggest, which is why I say I hardly knew him. We have thousands of members."

"He was active in the union?" Pauline asked.

"I wouldn't say that," Temperley replied. "He was just one of us. He wasn't an official, certainly not an activist."

"Harry Common didn't come to Durham that night to meet you or any of the others, did he?"

He shrugged. "Not to meet me, that I can tell you. As to the others, you'll have to ask them." He gestured to the group of men suspiciously watching them talk.

Pauline stepped toward them and said, "Did any of you arrange to meet Harry Common the night he died? I'm trying to set Harry's mother's mind at rest, you see. She doesn't understand what he was doing in Durham or why he would be fighting with anyone."

The men's expressions were sullen and for the first time she thought she saw the link she'd imagined may well be true. Their responses were uniformly negative, only she wasn't convinced.

Feeling she was getting nowhere and that they were now on their guard; Pauline thanked them and walked across the wet grass to ask the policeman, who was also watching her suspiciously, what he knew.

He, apparently, knew nothing. He hadn't been on duty at the cathedral on the night when the Gospels were taken in for observation, and he didn't know which officer was. Pauline didn't believe that last part but understood his reluctance; no one likes a snitch. She returned to her car relieved she'd at least managed to talk to the union men without a scene.

As she reached her car, a thought entered her head. She checked her watch. Almost seven-thirty, the viewing was ending. She might, if she waited, see the process for transferring the book to the police van on its way to the bank. When would that be? When you're lost, ask a policeman, she was always being told as a child and this seemed good advice tonight.

Pauline retraced her steps back to the constable on duty and asked. Around eight was his answer and Pauline returned to her car to wait in the relative comfort of its interior.

Before eight, she noticed the protesters gathering at a side door of the cathedral. A police van drove up and parked outside the wall that circled the property. She left her car and hurried over to watch.

She was just in time. The door opened and two burly policemen stepped out and created a channel through the mob of protesters. They parted amicably enough, and two security guards exited the building, one carrying what looked like a large, metal attaché case. She smiled to see it was now chained securely to the guard's wrist. The workingman's briefcase, indeed. The case was about eighteen inches long, twelve inches wide, and maybe six inches thick, presumably made of steel, painted black with silver fittings. It looked very ordinary, though she suspected the fittings and steel were not the regular metal of a case of this kind. The locks, too, were more substantial than those usually seen on briefcases or attaché cases. Still, they weren't exotic locks. They could be found in many industrial supply catalogs, she was sure.

The two guards, escorted by the two officers, made their way quickly to the van where two additional officers waited. The guards and the attaché case entered the back of the van, the doors closed, the police drivers re-entered the van and it drew away from the curb and merged into the stream of traffic on the road.

As Pauline returned to her own car, she reflected on her earlier conversation with Ramsay. What she'd just watched, and its mirror image when the van reached the bank, were the sensible time to steal the Gospels. Overpower the police and guards, or hold them up with guns, and drive off with the Gospels. Why wait until they were safe in the bank vault?

The best answer she could think of, as she made her way home, was the robbers didn't want any violence. They didn't want the possibility of a brave officer or guard fighting back, for example. This was very much an elegant crime. The kind the press was now calling a white-collar crime rather than the rougher, cruder crimes that upset the public. Did that mean these criminals were a more sensitive kind of people? Or did they just understand life would be easier lifting the Gospels from the bank vault overnight?

As she parked in the drive and prepared to enter the house, Pauline decided it did mean a better type of criminal, which probably meant the bank robbers and the so-called poverty action group weren't guilty. It had to be the gentry, an art dealer maybe, or sad to say, someone like Harry Common.

Chapter Fourteen

RAMSAY IN THE ART WORLD

THE BRIEFING ROOM was full as Ramsay entered and found a place at the back of the crowd. He'd worked too long with his small team, and been in charge too long, to be happy at this assignment.

The Scotland Yard man with his two juniors entered the room, and the meeting began. It ran along familiar lines, with updates from the night shift followed by the boss laying out what was to be done today. Ramsay found himself given the job of interviewing a sly customer he'd interviewed on more than one occasion in the past. A Newcastle art dealer called Julian Graystoke. At least that meant he'd be home in Newcastle at the end of the day and not stuck fighting traffic to get home on the Great North Road in rush hour.

To be sure his plan for the afternoon traffic avoidance worked, Ramsay spent the morning reading case files and researching the religious art scene in police files and then at the Durham Library. After a pub lunch of steak pie and chips, he drove slowly back north, over the Tyne Bridge. With a sigh of relief, he was back in Newcastle. He'd never cared for foreign travel and County Durham was as far as he was prepared to go. He knew this was crazy for he and his then new bride had traveled down from Ayrshire to take up his posting in Newcastle just before the war. He'd even traveled home to Scotland to visit family and friends before his wife and family's death. He hadn't minded traveling then. Now it felt like abandoning them, even though he rarely visited the grave.

He parked his car immediately outside the door of the small gallery, which was easy to do. The gallery was on a quiet side alley off Grainger Street and there was little traffic. He stood for a moment outside, just observing. Through the window, he could see Graystoke trying to entice a well-to-do man into buying a hideous, in Ramsay's opinion, abstract painting in varying shades of black, if that were possible, which Ramsay knew it shouldn't be but that's what it looked like.

When the prospective buyer left, empty-handed but promising to return, Ramsay had stepped inside the shop and asked, "Mr. Graystoke, may I have a word?"

"Inspector," Graystoke paused, thought for a moment, then brightened and said, "Ramsay. My memory grows worse with every passing day." He held up his hand to prevent Ramsay interjecting, before adding, "As I've told you and your colleagues on many occasions, whatever it is you're looking for, I don't know where it is."

"But you might know someone who might know where it is," Ramsay said.

Graystoke sighed, somewhat theatrically. "Inspector, please, rid your mind of the idea that because you don't like or understand the art I sell, it follows that I'm a crook."

"I don't assume dealers in anything are crooks, Mr. Graystoke. I do assume thieves will likely search out buyers for their loot and dealers are people they may approach. That's where you would assist the police with their enquiries as a good citizen would."

"Very well," Graystoke said. "I presume it's the Lindisfarne Gospels you're looking for?"

Ramsay tut-tutted. "Not at all. Those were only taken off display to preserve their safety. I'm sure you heard the news."

"I did," Graystoke said, "and like anyone in the business, I assumed the book was stolen and a replica will have been put in its place."

"I don't say that what you're saying is true, but there was a robbery at a house where valuable art works were stolen. Have you been approached to handle the sale of any valuable pieces?"

"Inspector, look around my gallery. I sell mainly modern art from young upcoming artists. I don't deal in ancient religious artifacts or old masters."

"I remember you sold a priceless Ming vase some years ago," Ramsay reminded him.

"I did, and if you recall, it was an heirloom from a friend's estate and all entirely above board on my account."

"I do recall. I also recall that the vase didn't belong to the family that sold it," Ramsay said.

"And therein lies the harassment I've received ever since," Graystoke said. "Neither I nor the beneficiaries of the estate knew it had been stolen decades before. We were innocent of any wrongdoing, but the police have considered me a fence for stolen goods from that day on."

"I see it more that we find you as a valuable resource to be tapped when there's a question of dodgy art being moved in the neighborhood."

"Perhaps I should get a police medal or commendation for being such a valuable resource, Inspector."

Ramsay smiled grimly. "I think that may be a step too far. After all, how valuable would you be to us if every crook in the county knew you were our valuable resource?"

"It might be a lot better for me if they did."

"It may be a lot worse," Ramsay said. "You know how criminal types treat people who betray them. Be careful what you wish for, Mr. Graystoke."

Graystoke visibly paled. "I haven't been approached by anyone about the Gospels." He paused before adding "Or any interesting art pieces and I haven't heard of anyone else being approached."

"Who might be a buyer if a treasure such as the Gospels were to come on the market?"

"Really, Inspector," Graystoke said. "Many collectors might like to have something like that in their collection, but it doesn't mean they would buy the artifact knowing it to be stolen."

"I understand," Ramsay said. "I'm not asking you to finger someone, just suggest who I might talk to among the local art world and who might be approached."

Graystoke's discomfort grew even more apparent as he wrestled with providing a name or risking Ramsay telling the world he helped out the police. At last, he said, "Sir Arthur Warkworth would be my best guess."

"Is he a customer of yours?"

Graystoke laughed. "He buys in more elevated circles than my poor gallery, Inspector. I just know he collects religious items, such as icons. He would probably welcome a western Christian artifact such as the Lindisfarne Gospels — or even some old masters."

"Thank you, Mr. Graystoke," Ramsay said. "You've

been most helpful." He turned to go, then stopped to add, "Remember what I said. The Gospels are not missing. Though it's possible some other equally valuable treasure is."

He left the gallery and returned to his car. It would be a pleasure to talk to Sir Arthur again. What was it about collectors that made him so suspicious? After all, as a child he'd briefly collected stamps before losing interest. That probably explained it; he was just jealous of the more committed personality.

As Sir Arthur lived north of the Tyne, and that meant he wouldn't be stuck on the bridge in traffic going home, Ramsay decided to visit him without phoning ahead. It sometimes paid to catch people off guard.

When Inspector Ramsay was finally shown into the study of Warkworth Hall, after a longer than was polite wait in an anteroom, Sir Arthur Warkworth was as little pleased to see Ramsay as Ramsay was to see him. Their paths had only crossed once before, and it was on a case such as this where a valuable collectible had gone missing from a great house at which Sir Arthur had been a recent guest.

"Am I to understand the Lindisfarne Gospels are missing, Inspector?" Warkworth asked.

'No, Sir Arthur," Ramsay replied. "Only that a valuable treasure is missing and we're working to retrieve it as quietly as we can. To spare the owner's blushes, you understand."

"What kind of treasure?" Warkworth asked suspiciously.

Ramsay, who had not been invited to sit, sat. "I'm not at liberty to say," he replied. "It would reveal the owners."

"Just a coincidence it happened when the Gospels were removed from public view, eh?"

"Not at all, we think the theft happened some time before, but the owners only reported it on their return from abroad," Ramsay said. "So not a coincidence, more a sharp operator taking advantage of an owner being away."

Sir Arthur snorted. "I suspect the owners took advantage of recent events to muddy the waters. Had you thought of that?"

"Very ingenious, Sir Arthur," Ramsay said amicably. "We need you in the force."

Not sure if he was being mocked, Sir Arthur said, "Well, as I say, it's something to consider."

"It is indeed, sir," Ramsay replied, "particularly with this scurrilous rumor going around about the Gospels being stolen."

"You're saying the genuine article was returned to display in the cathedral, not a replica brought up from London?"

"That's correct," Ramsay said. "You can view it in the knowledge you're seeing the real thing."

"Oh, I already saw it the first day," Warkworth said. "I was at the reception event."

Of course, you were, you old fraud, Ramsay thought, but said, "I take it you haven't been approached recently about a possible purchase of a valuable art work?"

"Not at all," Warkworth said, his expression displaying his anger that the police should think he would keep something like that from them.

"And you've never heard of anyone else being approached?"

"Inspector, if I'd heard anything I'd have contacted the police, I assure you."

Ramsay met his gaze evenly. Warkworth's bluster didn't make him forget that previous occasion they'd spoken and how long it had taken Warkworth to come forward with the knowledge of a crime.

"Then I won't take up any more of your time, Sir Arthur. I'll leave my card, so you'll know where and who to call if you do hear of anything." Ramsay smiled, placing the card on Warkworth's desk. "Good day. I'll see myself out."

Warkworth pulled a bell cord. The bell jangled somewhere in the depths of the house.

"Weston will see you out, Inspector. It's a big house and easy to get lost in all the corridors."

The study door opened, and the butler entered the room.

"Inspector Ramsay is leaving, Weston," Warkworth said coldly.

Weston led him directly to the front door, which was his job, but Ramsay wondered what he might have seen had he wandered down some, or all, of those corridors Sir Arthur had mentioned.

As the door of the Hall closed behind him, Ramsay grinned. Did he believe Warkworth any more than he believed Graystoke? Two peas in a pod and nothing to choose between them was his final decision. He drove slowly back into town and the quiet of his own house.

Chapter Fifteen

PAULINE AND RAMSAY DEBRIEF

AFTER A LIGHT SUPPER, Ramsay phoned Pauline.

"Good evening, Inspector. How can I help you?"

"I've been interviewing likely fences and collectors today," Ramsay said. "It was dull and unproductive. Are you having any success?"

"Not really," Pauline said, "I met the protesters this evening and I'm getting a measure of those who might be involved."

"Does any of that measuring point in a direction?"

"No," Pauline replied. "It mainly just confirms my prejudices. I don't like union men. They're intimidating and I think deliberately so."

He laughed. "So, if you come forward with evidence they're linked to Harry's death or the robbery I should be careful to check it out before sending it on to my bosses?"

It was Pauline's turn to laugh. "You should, Inspector, but believe me I will have checked myself more than once before suggesting they're involved because I know my own feelings aren't neutral."

"I'm pleased to hear it."

"The union men did know Harry Common, though," Pauline said. "And if he came to Durham to meet someone, why not them?"

"Did you ask them?"

"I did," Pauline said. "They said he wasn't meeting them. I don't believe them."

"But you're prejudiced, Miss Riddell," Ramsay reminded her.

"I know," Pauline said. "I'll have to find proof they're lying before I bring it to you as a serious possibility."

"If you and Poppy hadn't fallen out, you could have had a news photographer snap them and then ask the bar staff at the Wheatsheaf."

"I'm going to do that using the photos in the papers," Pauline said. "They aren't great, but they may be good enough."

"Be careful when you go," Ramsay said. "They may be in there when you arrive and realize what you're doing."

"I'll be in the ladies lounge, Inspector, and none of them would be seen dead in there. I think I'll be safe." She paused before asking, "Do you think your fence and collector would be more willing to talk to a celebrity sleuth than an old police inspector?"

"Hey," Ramsay said, "less of the *old*, young lady. I'm in the prime of life. But your suggestion isn't completely unlikely. How would you approach them?"

"You tell me," Pauline replied. "I wouldn't have heard about them from the protesters or Mrs. Common, that's for sure."

Ramsay considered for a moment. "What about Sir Robert Lauriston? Might he have suggested the dealers, for example?"

"He didn't, likely because I didn't ask him," Pauline said. "Maybe, I should. I'll phone him the moment we end this call."

Sir Robert, however, when asked, declined to mention any dealers or collectors who he knew might be interested in stolen antiquities, adding, "I understood the Gospels are back on display now the conservator has approved it, so I don't understand why you'd want to know who might buy a stolen art item."

"My friend Inspector Ramsay is working on a house robbery where valuable art went missing. He asked me to keep my ear to the ground while I talked to people about Harry Common, that's all."

Sir Robert laughed. "Inspector Ramsay must have a strange idea of the Common family's life if he thinks they were into selling valuable artworks. I doubt Harry, though an educated man in so many practical fields, would know a masterpiece from a mantelpiece."

"I understand your loyalty to your friend, Sir Robert," Pauline said, "but he did know something about master-pieces, or at least antiquities. He knew of the Gospels, for example, and he was in Durham on business his mother knew little about. I'm not saying he stole anything, only that he may have become caught up in something he didn't know was criminal and was killed when he found out and tried to back out."

Sir Robert was quiet for a moment. Pauline waited expectantly.

"Certainly, Harry would want out if he found himself involved in something criminal," he said slowly.

Pauline waited, unwilling to distract him as his thoughts went down the direction she'd pointed him in.

"You have to understand, I know nothing against these

two individuals, Miss Riddell," he said at last. "Only, I hear from others that they sail close to the wind on some deals. There's a gallery in Newcastle, Graystoke's. That might be somewhere to start." He paused.

"You mentioned two names," Pauline prompted him when he had paused for too long.

"I'm even more uncomfortable about this one," Sir Robert said. "He and I have been rivals when buying many artifacts down the years and I don't like him. My giving you his name may be pure prejudice on my part and that I don't like."

"There must be a reason you don't like him," Pauline said. "Some instinct warning you?"

He laughed. "We're too quick to assign wrongdoing to people we don't like, in my experience, but I will give you his name. Sir Arthur Warkworth. He may know if there's anything out there for sale."

"I won't tell him I got his name from you," Pauline said. "I don't want to start some kind of vendetta between you two."

"Oh, he would do the same to me," Sir Robert said. "As you'll find if you meet him."

Chapter Sixteen

PAULINE MEETS SIR ARTHUR

PAULINE FOUND, to her continuing surprise, that her fame opened doors that once would have been shut tight had she approached them before. In this case, it was the doors of Warkworth Hall, when she called and asked if she could talk to Sir Arthur. It seemed even a local bigwig like Sir Arthur kept in touch with current events enough to want to speak to the famous Miss Riddell.

When she reached the Hall that following evening at the appointed hour, she pulled on the impressive lion-headed doorbell handle and waited. It wasn't long before the door opened, for which she was thankful. It was a raw, wintry day with a sharp wind blowing in from the sea.

"Miss Riddell?" the servant asked.

He was such a top-drawer kind of fellow, Pauline surmised he must be the butler.

"Yes," she said. "I have an appointment to meet with Sir Arthur."

He stepped aside and gestured her to enter, which she thankfully did. Her headscarf and muffler weren't proof enough against that wind. How is it, she thought, that the Gulf Stream is supposed to warm the waters around us, yet the wind blowing over the sea seems to come straight from the Arctic?

"This way, Miss Riddell," the man said, leading her across a wide entrance hall toward a paneled corridor at the farther side. "Sir Arthur is expecting you."

The room she was led into, the butler announcing her with such grave solemnity she wanted to laugh, was a library-cum-study with dark wooden bookshelves against the walls and comfy leatherbound chairs and chaise-longue for furniture. A mannish room. Somewhere for Sir Arthur to relax and away from Lady Warkworth and children, if there were any.

"Good evening, Miss Riddell," Warkworth said, examining her keenly.

She hoped he wasn't too disappointed to find the famous Miss Riddell was no more than an office girl.

"Good evening, Sir Arthur," Pauline said. She wasn't sure of the correct mode of address, but it was what the butler had called him, so it seemed safe enough. "Thank you for seeing me."

His expression was benign; however, his eyes were sharp and wary. "I couldn't miss the opportunity of meeting someone so famous. Your name has been all over the news lately."

Pauline smiled. "The local papers are always eager for local success stories," she said, "and I've been their good news when the local football teams aren't doing so well. At least, that's how it seems to me."

He nodded. "Still, I ask myself, what does the famous sleuth want with me?"

"It's a delicate subject," Pauline said. "My good friend

Inspector Ramsay told me of a valuable art treasure that's missing, and he suggested I might assist him with his enquiries."

He looked genuinely shocked. "You're not saying the Lindisfarne Gospels have been stolen, are you?"

Pauline shook her head. "They aren't the only treasure in the north, Sir Arthur, though I do realize the coincidence of them being withdrawn from public view for a time might lead you to think that."

"I'm glad it isn't the Gospels," he said. "I was hoping that, if this visit to the north went well, we could expect to see them home more often in the future. People here need something to lift their spirits, something to remind them we've been important for thousands of years, not just the last one hundred."

Pauline nodded. "I'm behind you on that, Sir Arthur. People do need to be reminded. They're very down in the dumps right now. Nothing seems to be recovering from the war as quickly as we all hoped."

He frowned. "Where are my manners. Please sit down, Miss Riddell." He gestured to an armchair across a low exquisitely polished table from his own seat.

Pauline sat. "The reason I'm here is not because I thought you have this missing item," she said. "I was told you're a well-known collector of art and antiquities and I thought you might hear of stories about such an item."

He laughed. "Dealers and collectors keep very quiet about important finds. The collector doesn't want to have competing bids and the dealer doesn't want to break trust with a favored client."

"Oh," Pauline said. "I'm not familiar with this world and I'd hoped insiders would hear things."

"We do, sometimes," Sir Arthur said. "If the collector

decides not to buy or is too hesitant and the dealer hunts around for an alternative, for example. Usually, though, it's only if the deal isn't going to happen that we hear."

"Then I'll be blunt, Sir Arthur," Pauline said. "Could you suggest any names of who might know of a private sale of this criminal kind?"

"This is plain speaking, Miss Riddell. I don't move in criminal circles, and I hope any bent dealer would know not to approach me." His expression darkened and his tone was terse.

"Please believe me, Sir Arthur. I've approached you because I was assured you were a scrupulously honest man. I'm not trying to insinuate you're not. I'm just looking for help in a world I know nothing about."

His mood lightened again. "I understand. There are local collectors we hear rumors about, of course. Only, they aren't generally foolish enough to show other people treasures they've come by ambiguously, shall we say."

Pauline sighed dramatically. Her little-girl-lost routine wasn't opening his tongue so far, maybe she needed to increase the volume.

"Is there anyone you could suggest I talk to who might have a wider circle of friends in the art world?"

"You make it difficult for me, Miss Riddell. Any name I give you now will be tainted. You're going to assume I think they're crooked and that isn't the case. I don't know anyone, dealer or collector, who I think would be in possession of stolen property."

"Of course not," Pauline said. "I wouldn't imagine any such thing. Only someone might have heard something and unless I can talk to them, they may not know the object was not being offered for sale honestly. You see my dilemma?"

"So long as we're clear," Sir Arthur said. "I'm not

suggesting either of these two people are in any way involved with criminal activity, now or at any other time."

"That is very clear," Pauline said, leaning forward hopefully.

"There's a dealer in Newcastle, Purcell Antiques, who often has pieces that come to him from estate sales or private collectors, rather than through the usual trade channels. He might have heard something or been approached. I've no doubt he would reject anything he knew to be stolen but he might have been approached."

Pauline noted the name in her diary and asked, "And?"

"Sir Robert Lauriston is a well-known collector of antiquities. If this missing item is a local antiquity, he would be approached, you can be sure. However, there's no doubt in my mind he would also refuse to have anything to do with stolen property."

"Thank you, Sir Arthur," Pauline said. "Is there anything else I should know?"

"You should know that if I am approached about buying this mysterious missing piece, I will inform the police immediately."

Pauline thanked him for his time and was escorted to the door by the silent butler. She couldn't decide if the butler was so stiff because he thought this work beneath his lofty station, after all in the good old days there would have been a footman to attend the door, or whether he just didn't approve of ordinary people on what he considered his territory.

Outside, it was raining, a cold, solid downpour that meant the quick run across the open ground to her car left her woolen coat and the jacket beneath soaked. It brought an end to her day's sleuthing. If she didn't get out of these wet clothes soon, she'd have a chill for the rest of the week.

Later, after changing and warming herself before the fire, Pauline phoned Ramsay. "Good evening, Inspector," she began as soon as she heard the handset picked up.

'Good evening, Miss Riddell," Ramsay said. "Did you learn anything from Warkworth?"

"I suspect no more than you did," Pauline said. "He did suggest I talk to a Peter Purcell and Sir Robert Lauriston. Have you spoken to them?

"To Mr. Purcell, yes," Ramsay replied. "He's one of the people we approach first whenever there's anything odd going on in artistic circles, along with Julian Graystoke."

"He's known to the police," Pauline said, laughing.

"They both are but to be fair there's never been anything proven against either of them."

"I'll do some window shopping at his gallery tomorrow lunch time," Pauline said, "and visit them in the evenings or whenever they're open. What did they tell you?"

"That they knew nothing about any missing artifacts," Ramsay replied.

Pauline said, smiling, "Can I tell you something funny about my meetings with Sir Robert and Sir Arthur?"

Ramsay laughed. "What was that?"

"I asked Sir Robert for a local collector who might be approached by someone selling stolen art treasures and he hummed and hawed before giving me Sir Arthur's name, stressing how innocent he believed him to be. I asked Sir Arthur the same question and he gave me Sir Robert's name without a moment's hesitation, as Sir Robert had said he would. What would you make of that exchange?"

"That they don't like each other very much," Ramsay said. "We don't know anything shady about Sir Robert; he's a well-liked local man with business interests. He was a mine owner before the pits were nationalized, is a collector of art and antiquities, and he's a Justice of the Peace."

"Sir Arthur assured me he was an all-round good chap," Pauline said, smiling to herself, "as Sir Robert assured me of Sir Arthur. It's perplexing."

"That would be because they're rivals in business, collecting, and politics," Ramsay said. "They're both on their respective County Councils and often disagree, I'm told. I have no direct knowledge for I take no interest in such matters unless it's police business."

"Of the two, I liked Sir Robert best," Pauline said, "but he has a grievance over his mine being taken from him and that makes me nervous."

Ramsay laughed. "Liking people isn't a good guide when investigating, Miss Riddell. Now what are your next steps?"

"Hold your horses there, Inspector," Pauline cried. "I haven't finished this line of enquiry yet."

"You don't want to be twiddling your thumbs while you wait to talk to those dealers," Ramsay said. "You should re-visit the protesters tomorrow. The church ladies are holding a vigil."

"I'll take some time to think about my next steps, Inspector. I got drenched visiting Sir Arthur and I mean to warm through beside the fire tonight."

"That will give you time to think how you'll attack those dealers," Ramsay answered.

"Even you have begun to take on the Task Force way of speaking, Inspector. I don't plan to 'attack' anyone."

He laughed, harshly. "It's true. So many of my colleagues are ex-military. Their way of speaking seeps into my thoughts and words too."

"I will call tomorrow evening, Inspector, and tell you

what I learn from Mr. Graystoke, if you'll give me directions to his gallery, or from the protesters if I go there. I'll start with him because Sir Robert gave me his name and I trust Sir Robert more than I trust Warkworth."

Ramsay laughed and tut-tutted at her bluntness, while he searched for the address. Pauline copied the address and directions Ramsay provided and hung up the phone.

Pauline returned to the living room where Mrs. Bertram looked up from her knitting and asked, "How is Inspector Ramsay?"

"I didn't ask," Pauline replied. "I imagine he's well."

"The time we met, he struck me as a sad man," Mrs. Bertram said. "There's some awful loss in his life, I'm sure."

Pauline frowned. "With the recent wars, we all have some of that inside us." It was true and yet she couldn't help noticing her own loss, the death of her fiancé Stephen in Korea, was already fading and it was only months ago. She sometimes felt living with Stephen's parents was all that was keeping it alive.

"It's true, we do," Mrs. Bertram said, looking across the room to where her husband was studiously reading his book, pretending they weren't talking about the loss all three shared. "What is it Inspector Ramsay wants you to do now, dear?"

Pauline was always irritated by Mrs. Bertram's unshakeable assumption that Ramsay told Pauline what to do but she answered calmly, "He suggested I might learn something more about what's going on by talking to some art dealers, Julian Graystoke and Peter Purcell. Have either of you been to their galleries?"

"Oh dear," Mrs. Bertram said, grimacing at the thought. "Art dealers. Is one of them the person Inspector Ramsay thinks killed that poor man? I wish you wouldn't get involved with murders. Inspector Ramsay should have more sense."

"Harry Common was the victim, not the perpetrator," Pauline said, almost crossly. "And we don't know it was a murder yet. And Mr. Graystoke, who I shall visit tomorrow, is a reputable businessman, so far as anyone knows."

"I read about that man's death in the paper," Mr. Bertram said, suddenly taking notice. "The article said he died in a fight outside a public house. Surely, that's only manslaughter?"

"And that's all I know too," Pauline said. "Inspector Ramsay just felt it was a coincidence he died so soon after the Martin's bank robbery. He thought a woman's touch may get more information about Harry than a policeman's touch. But tomorrow, I'm talking to a man who sells art. I suspect the Inspector thinks a woman's touch would help there too."

Bertram nodded. "You might do better," he said. "Especially, if he thought you were just a customer."

"Wouldn't that be dishonest, dear?" Mrs. Bertram asked. "He would be very unhappy with Pauline if at some point he realized she was a police spy."

"I'm not a police spy!" Pauline cried.

"Well, he would think so if you presented yourself as a customer and then proceeded to interrogate him," Mrs. Bertram said, bluntly. "I can't think that wise."

"You never told us how the meeting with the dead man's mother went, Pauline," Mr. Bertram said, feeling a change of subject may be needed.

"It went well," Pauline said. "I just didn't learn anything that could help me explain what is going on."

"What did you hope to hear?" Mr. Bertram asked.

"I hoped she might know who he was going to see in Durham and why."

"Would a mother really say anything that might reflect badly on her dead son, though?" Mr. Bertram asked. "What do you think, dear?" he added, looking at his wife.

"I'm sure I don't know," Mrs. Bertram said, severely. "No child of mine would find themselves being investigated by the police."

"If a mother thought it may get him, and her, justice, she might," Pauline said. "After all, robbing banks isn't a capital offence, and no one should die for it."

"Well do be careful, Pauline," Mrs. Bertram said. "Working people can be very rough if they believe you're not acting in their best interest."

Pauline smiled. She had first-hand experience of that and, though her beliefs made her want to dismiss the suggestion, she knew she couldn't entirely. "I will behave toward Mrs. Common and the others I talk to as I would any person. I'm sure I shall be safe. Their bark really is worse than their bite."

Chapter Seventeen

RAMSAY AND CROKER

THE SCOTLAND YARD man finished his speech intended to rouse the team's energy and passed over to his deputy the task of handing out the jobs for the day. As they'd never asked for input from Ramsay on these assignments, he was always expecting his assignment to be completely wrong for him. So far, however, they'd surprised him and given him tasks that aligned with his rank, his local knowledge, and his expertise.

Once again, he was pleasantly surprised.

"Ramsay," the deputy said, "the local plods have identified a villain in connection with the bank robbery. We've considered the possible handling of the stolen Gospels in Newcastle. Now we need to see if the whole theft was planned from there. That's yours. Start by talking to Inspector Watson of the Durham robbery investigation. He'll fill you in."

Ramsay left the room and went in search of his contact in the Durham police headquarters. It was a fine day and only short walk, but it still gave him enough time to think.

His thoughts should have been about the case but mainly they were about the contrast between his own city beat and this one.

Newcastle was an industrial city and had been for a hundred and fifty years or more. Its buildings, even those built of local stone centuries before industrialization, were blackened by soot from the thousands of coal burning fires. Everything reeked of coal soot. By the end of a day, blowing one's nose left black marks on your handkerchief. Rain was black by the time it reached the ground and the rivulets that ran down the road to drains were like streams of tar. Smoke from those thousands of chimneys often didn't rise much above the level of roof tops, swirling in the mist and wind, blackening clothes and any washing hung out to dry on lines. It was a dirty old town -- and he loved it.

Durham wasn't industrial. It was a county town, a university town and had the feel of an Oxford or Cambridge of the north. Its old stone buildings, the castle, the cathedral, and the university, were the color of the local stone; they looked like they'd grown out of the ground rather than being built by man. There were, of course, parts of Newcastle that were leafy and green. There were parts of Durham that weren't. That was the difference. For Ramsay, Durham was a nice place to visit but it didn't feel like home at all.

He arrived at the police station and learned from Inspector Watson the tenuous link they'd discovered.

"You might recognize some of these names, Inspector," Watson said, as he wrapped up his exchange.

Ramsay nodded. "I do," he said, "but I'd be surprised to find they were the brains behind the whole affair. Hired help, I'd say."

Watson grinned. "That's what your colleagues said when I talked to them on the phone yesterday."

"If they're involved, I don't see any need for me to pursue this," Ramsay said.

"They made it plain you were their representative on this, and they were not going to become involved."

Ramsay laughed. He could imagine his colleagues' reply. "Then I'll take this," he waved the file he'd been handed, "and I'll get started. I'll liaise with you on what I find."

Outside, he took the scenic route back to his car. He intended to do all his investigating back in Newcastle after lunch, that way he could go straight home. This was becoming a very pleasant change from his usual life. He'd thought for some time he needed to get out more.

A leisurely drive back to Newcastle brought him to lunch time and the seediest pub on the docks. Normally, it would never have been Ramsay's first choice. However, that's where he took himself for that's where he'd find his man. As he ordered a pint, he surveyed the clientele who, in turn, eyed him with distaste he could practically feel.

"Will Ted Croker be in today?" he asked the bar tender as he paid for his drink

The barman shrugged. "Couldn't say. He doesn't tell me where he's going."

"I'll have a seat over in the corner," Ramsay said. "You'll tell him I'd like a word if he shows up, won't you."

"If he does," the man said and turned to serve another customer.

The bench Ramsay sat on was grubby, sticky even. Cleanliness wasn't what brought people to this pub. He sipped his beer, watching the men entering, leaving, talking briefly with friends, and always eyeing Ramsay like he was a bad smell in the room. Finally, after about fifteen minutes, Ramsay's patience was rewarded. Croker entered, got a drink at the bar and, after a brief discussion with the barman, crossed the floor to confront Ramsay.

"What do you want, Ramsay?"

"To talk," Ramsay said. "Just to talk."

Croker sat on the stool across the small, round, visibly sticky table from Ramsay and said, "That's nice. The weather is it, or your health?" He was a heavy-set man who'd been an amateur boxer in his younger days. The war had put an end to any hope of going professional and he'd been too old to continue when he was finally de-mobilized.

Ramsay smiled thinly. "It's about a bank robbery that happened in Durham the other day."

"I heard about that. Nought to do with me. I'm an honest man, though you people can't believe it."

"Being in the scrap metal business, you must hear a lot of stories. I thought maybe you'd heard something about this one."

Croker laughed. "If a car is nicked, or lead off a church roof, I'll grant you there's a chance a scrap metal merchant might be approached. Unless these robbers ran off with a lot of easily melted coins, I don't think they'll be bothering me."

Again, Ramsay smiled. There was no humor in it. "Nevertheless, scrap dealers may be asked to provide an old car as a getaway vehicle, for example, or to melt down some gold and silver jewelry, for instance. Nothing like that comes to mind?"

Croker shook his head. "Nought like that."

"And yet, we hear rumors…" Ramsay left the sentence unfinished.

"You can't believe everything you hear," Croker said. "You should know that."

"I do," Ramsay said. "However, it's the nature of my business that I must listen and investigate and here I am."

"Look," Croker said. "I'm a local businessman, not a bank robber. What more can I say?"

"You might say if you've heard any of these rumors."

Croker frowned. "Why would I have heard?"

"Businessmen need to keep their ears to the ground," Ramsay said.

"About business," Croker said. "Not about crimes. Scrap metal businesses do sometimes get the proceeds of crime dumped in our yards; we can't know where everything comes from. But loot from a bank job? Hardly. Use your head, Inspector."

"As I said," Ramsay replied. "We have to follow up on what we hear."

"Someone somewhere is setting me up," Croker said. "Pointing a finger my way so you won't look in their direction. I suggest you think who that might be. I'm sure you know who the real crooks in this town are."

"You couldn't suggest who might be pointing at you?"

"Nay," Croker said. "The kind of people who rob banks with explosives aren't the sort of people I want to offend. My business isn't bomb-proof."

"So, you did hear explosives were involved?"

"Ask anyone on the street," Croker said. "Word gets around, even when the papers don't print it."

"You didn't hear where the explosives came from, did you?"

"No, I didn't," Croker said. "Now, I've said I know nothing about any of this in as many ways as I can. It's been nice talking with you again, Inspector, but I think we should stop here."

"Sure," Ramsay said. "After all, I know where to find you if any more questions come to mind."

"It's a pity you didn't come to my office today," Croker said. "Instead of making the pub unpleasant for its customers."

"You know how it is," Ramsay said. "A message must be sent and sometimes it has to be delivered personally."

Croker's face darkened. "What message is that?"

"That I want to know about the Durham bank robbery and anyone who has information about it only has to get in touch."

Croker laughed harshly. "And you think they will?"

"As I said, you know how it is," Ramsay replied evenly. "Someone with a grievance, someone who didn't get enough, someone who tells someone, and that second someone needs cash. It always happens."

Croker rose. "If any of those *someones* point a finger my way, you can take it from me they're lying." He walked away, placed his glass on the bar, nodded goodbye to the bartender, and left the pub.

Ramsay too finished his drink. Newcastle's famous Brown Ale wasn't his favorite drink, but it hit the spot, especially in a place so close to the heart of the city where local pride meant a lot. It also helped it was a bottled beer so there was no chance the barman might tamper with it as a warning to an unwelcome customer. He made his way out of the pub, every sense alert to a possible ambush. Nothing happened and he made his way back to his car, which he'd parked far enough away not to be 'accidentally' damaged.

He drove slowly along the road that backed the quayside. A small merchant ship was preparing to leave, smoke streaming from its funnel, adding to the smoke of the city. Men on deck were preparing to recover the heavy ropes tying the ship to the shore, while men on the dock unwound the ropes from the heavy iron bollards.

High up on the ship's bridge, officers watched the crew below readying the ship for leaving.

Ramsay thought how handy a port was for a criminal gang. The proceeds of a nighttime robbery could be bundled into a cargo case and out of the country without the loot ever seeing the light of day. He drove past the ship as it slowly pulled away from the quay. Was this ship carrying away the Durham haul or did one very like it do so yesterday? It hardly mattered. For now, he needed to be in his office when the call or calls came in. Whoever coined the phrase 'honor among thieves' wasn't in any police force, that was for sure.

Chapter Eighteen

PAULINE AT THE WHEATSHEAF

PAULINE WAITED PATIENTLY AS she listened to the phone ringing. It was only mid-afternoon, and she was hoping to catch Inspector Ramsay at home. His office had told her he'd gone to interview someone in Newcastle, which Pauline felt should be over by now.

Finally, he picked up. "Yes," he said gruffly.

"Good afternoon, Inspector," Pauline said. "I've decided not to attend the vigil or Graystoke's Gallery. I'm planning to visit the Wheatsheaf and talk to the staff. What can you tell me from the police investigation of the evening Harry Common died?"

Ramsay wondered a little about this change of direction, then decided not to ask why. "There's little to tell," he said, "as far as I can gather. Harry Common went there that evening, knowing no one. He spoke to a group of men in the pub. He left the pub and sometime soon after he was punched and died."

"There was no evidence at the scene?"

"None at all," Ramsay said. "The pathologist identified

that the man who hit him wore several heavy rings on his hand. Not a knuckleduster, exactly, but the next best thing."

"Wouldn't that be enough for an identification?" Pauline asked. "It sounds like something the assailant would have worn in fights before this one."

"Apparently, it wasn't enough, Miss Riddell, because they never found the man," Ramsay said. "Maybe the man had only just bought these rings. Or maybe he's never hit anyone with them before."

"He will have ditched the rings, you can be sure," Pauline said. That was a blow. "The local police did look at links to the robbery and the protesters, though?"

"They did and say they could see none," Ramsay said. "It may well just be a tragic accident, a street hold-up gone terribly wrong."

"And yet, coincidences," Pauline said. "We don't like them, do we, Inspector?"

"We do not, Miss Riddell. Maybe you can get something more out of the locals or staff at the Wheatsheaf than we did,"

"I'll certainly try," Pauline said, "though I'd hoped for something more to go on."

"Don't do anything foolish, Miss Riddell," Ramsay said. "Your heroics in the previous two cases were more than enough for me." He hung up.

For the next hour, Pauline glanced at her wristwatch every second minute. Investigating was all very well for Inspector Ramsay; it was his job. She, however, had a full-time job that kept her chained to a desk. She could only investigate outside of work. Her impatience was ameliorated when her boss, Dr. Enderby, came out of his office carrying his coat and briefcase.

"I'm going home, Pauline," he said, "taking my work with me. You can go too when you finish that report."

"I will," Pauline said. "I'm almost done. I'll leave it on your desk for the morning. Good night."

Her fingers flew over the keys as she wrapped up the final pages, placed them in a file folder, and dropped them on his desk. Minutes later, she was in her car and heading out of the factory gates to visit the pub where Harry Common died. By leaving early, she hoped to be there before the regulars arrived at the pub for their evening drink.

The Wheatsheaf was indeed practically empty when Pauline walked in. She ordered her sherry at the bar in the ladies lounge.

While the serving woman was turned away finding the sherry among the many bottles on the countertop, Pauline asked, "Were you working the night Harry Common died?"

The woman, middle-aged, blonde hair in curls, turned abruptly and said, "What?"

"Sorry," Pauline said, smiling. "I didn't mean to startle you. I'm Pauline Riddell, by the way. You may have heard of me."

The woman's expression suggested she had heard of Pauline and didn't approve. It looked like she might refuse to answer or deny she was working that night. Then her expression lightened. "You're that girl who solved those murders. Do you think that fella was murdered?"

Pauline shook her head. "I don't, but I do think it was odd. I spoke to his mother, and she says he never drank here."

"Aye, that's true enough. I never seen him here anyhow."

"I'm trying to set her mind at ease," Pauline said. "Knowing it really was just an accident, would help her come to terms with his death, you see."

"He never drank here but the man who punched him did," the woman said. "Though I ain't seen him here since that night."

"But you've seen the others?"

"Aye," she said. "They're in tonight, my bad luck. I don't even like serving them."

Pauline shifted her position along the bar to get a glimpse through a hatch to the saloon. Finally, she saw a group of men with backs to her, but their shapes were familiar. "The violent one isn't in, you say?"

The barmaid nodded.

"He's probably horrified at what happened and is staying away," Pauline said.

The woman laughed. "If he's horrified it's only because this time, he killed someone. He was allus starting trouble."

"With people who were new in the pub?" Pauline asked. "I know there are men who see the pub as theirs and don't care for strangers."

"Nay. He starts fights with anyone, that one. He's just that sort."

"Then it probably was an accident," Pauline said. "One of those stupid brawls men enjoy when they've drunk too much."

The woman frowned. "Maybe. Though I think there was more to it. I told the police so, too. Though not who the men were," she added hastily.

"In what sense?"

"The man who died," she said. "I'd never seen him in here, but he seemed to be known to the local men. Or at least, one or two of them anyway. He talked to them for a time before he left."

"The man who hit him, was he in the group?"

"He was and he left the pub right after the man who died," the woman said. "He came back in minutes later, white as a sheet asking for help. We phoned for an ambulance and the police, but it was too late."

"It does sound like he didn't mean to kill Harry Common," Pauline agreed. "He just meant to give him a message."

The woman nodded. "And yet the talk they'd all had seemed friendly enough. I don't understand it and that's a fact. There's more to it than meets the eye, as they say."

"It sounds like it," Pauline said. "Does the violent man wear rings?"

"Not so I've noticed," the woman said. "Why?"

"I just wondered. It might explain why Harry Common died if a heavy, ornate ring hit him at a weak spot."

The woman frowned. "Wait a bit," she said. "Let me ask Mr. Jobson. He does the saloon bar. He doesn't like me or his wife serving those lot." She stepped through the gap that separated the saloon serving area from the ladies lounge bar area.

Pauline heard a low conversation before the owner himself appeared. "You're the famous, or is that infamous, Miss Riddell," he said, grinning.

Pauline smiled. "I am she."

His voice, which had been low enough before, dropped to a whisper. "Alice said you'd asked about rings on the hand of the thug who drinks with the men through there."

Pauline nodded.

"Well, you didn't hear this from me or Alice, but he does

wear heavy rings sometimes. They look like those knuckle-dusters you see thugs wearing in gangster movies, only not joined together, you understand."

"Did you see them that night?"

He shook his head. "No, but I didn't look. It doesn't do to look at any of them too often or for too long. It makes them aggressive."

"Do you know their names?" Pauline asked.

"I know their first names only and even they're nick-names. The man we're talking about gets called Gently by the others."

"Gently!" Pauline cried, too loudly, then caught herself and whispered, "He doesn't sound gentle."

"They fancy themselves as socialist intellectuals. It's from that Dylan Thomas poem, you know the one, *do not go gentle into the night, rage, rage against the dying light* or however it goes."

"I see. Very amusing for them, I'm sure," Pauline said. "Now I only have to find someone brave enough to speak out against him, and them." She looked into Mr. Jobson's eyes, hoping to shame him into action. It was not to be.

"I wish you well with that, Miss Riddell. If, as seems likely, these people have killed once, you can be sure they won't hesitate to do it again to save their necks from the noose."

Pauline nodded. She understood, but it was a blow. Maybe giving Ramsay the name would get the police actively involved again and they would find some evidence. She thanked him and he and Alice swapped places again.

"Was Mr. Jobson able to help?" Alice asked quietly.

"I think so," Pauline said. "Was there anything else *you* thought odd that night?"

The woman shook her head.

"If you think of something," Pauline said, "here's my phone number. Please call me." She hoped Alice might say something on the phone she wouldn't say publicly in the bar.

Chapter Nineteen

PAULINE AND THE PROTESTERS

AFTER FINISHING HER SHERRY, Pauline walked from the pub to the cathedral. If the protesters were still there, she might learn something new. It was a bad night to be outside, Pauline thought, as she pulled her scarf tighter around her neck in an effort to stop the icy rain running down inside her clothes. Before she arrived at the cathedral, she was puzzled to hear singing. Men's voices singing an old folk song and women singing a hymn. When she realized what she was listening to, she laughed.

Rounding the corner and entering the cathedral grounds, she saw what she'd expected. Dressed in a motley collection of rainwear, old fishermen's waterproofs of the kind called 'sou'westers' predominating, the bearded, nationalists were indeed singing old local songs while the church ladies were rivaling them with hymns. At least it's all amicable, she thought as she approached Theresa, the church women's leader, who was conducting the woman's choir with extravagant arm flailing.

"Good evening," Pauline said, approaching her.

"Miss Riddell, how nice to see you again. Wait one moment, we're almost at the end." With a final flourish, she and the women ended with a solemn amen.

"If you could persuade the gentlemen to join you," Pauline said, "you'd have a winning choir, I think."

Theresa grinned. "They're heathens, sadly. Not even Protestants. They only know working and fighting songs, and also some songs we don't care to hear."

"Still no poverty activists tonight?" Pauline asked.

Theresa shook her head. "They're only here when there's a likelihood of the press showing up. I think they're frauds."

Now that the women were no longer singing, the men had stopped too and the only sound to be heard was the hum of traffic on the roads around the cathedral. It was a cold evening with a sky of heavy, fast-moving clouds dropping sudden showers, and an almost full moon appearing briefly when there was a break in them. The cathedral's bulk loomed above them, lit by nearby streetlamps and the dim lights inside seen through stained glass windows.

By comparison with the men's wild mix of waterproof clothes, the women were an orderly group clothed in Burberry mackintoshes, rubber wellington boots, and sheltering umbrellas.

"Who starts the singing?" Pauline asked.

"Originally, we started it by singing hymns to keep our bodies warm and our spirits up," Theresa said. "The men took it as a challenge. Now, either of us can start and the other answers the challenge. It's quite fun." She smiled, looking wistfully over at the bundled-up figures across the lawn.

"When the Gospels return to London, you should make it a memorial event," Pauline said, laughing.

"We could, couldn't we," Theresa said. "Stranger things have become local traditions in the past."

"I came to ask if any of your group knew Harry Common," Pauline said.

"As I mentioned when we spoke, I didn't see him," Theresa said. "Ask the others, if you have a photo or if they saw his photo in the paper maybe they'll recognize him."

None of the women remembered Harry, they assured Pauline. She hadn't expected they would. From all she'd learned, it was unlikely Harry had ever been part of the protests.

"Maybe ask over there," Theresa said. "Alf and his gang of ruffians may have seen him."

Pauline noted the fondness in Theresa's tone and knew the rivalry between the two sets of protesters had long since shifted into camaraderie. Solidarity wasn't just for workers, it seemed.

"I shall," Pauline said. "Thank you. I'll join you in a hymn after if I may."

"You'll be very welcome. If the ruffians let you leave. I warn you. They lack female company and will try to seduce you into staying."

Pauline laughed and thanked her for her advice. "Theresa, is the man called Alf Batey?"

"That's the one. Do you know him?"

Pauline shook her head. "No. I was just given his name as Mr. Batey."

She crossed the lawn and hailed the man she recognized from her previous visit.

"Good evening, Miss Riddell," he said. "You wisely escaped the clutches of the sirens over there with their melodious voices and evil ways. It's hard for a lonely traveler to escape them. Did you tie yourself to a mast like Odysseus?"

"Sirens only lure *men* to their doom," Pauline said. "Surely you remember that from schooldays."

"True, I had forgot," he said, grinning broadly. "So, what brings the intrepid Miss Riddell here again? More sleuthing?"

"Yes, more sleuthing. I'm still looking into the death of Harry Common. Are any of you regulars at the Wheatsheaf?"

"I'm not, but we can ask the others." He turned to them and said, "Listen up! Miss Riddell has a question."

Pauline repeated the question. There was a general shaking of heads.

"Harry Common died outside the Wheatsheaf on Market Street," Pauline said. "Do any of you ever drink there?"

Once again, there was a general shaking of heads and muttered noes, though Pauline felt one or two looked uneasy.

"Are none of you Durham men?"

A man spoke. "I've been to the Wheatsheaf more than once, but it isn't my regular pub." With the ice broken, others agreed they too had been there occasionally.

"I was just there," Pauline said. "I saw some of the poverty action men there, at least, I think it was them."

"They're the reason it isn't my local," the man who'd first spoken said, laughing.

"If they're there all the time, they must be local men," Pauline said.

"Aye, they are, more's the pity."

"They give the pub a bad name, I see," Pauline said, smiling.

"They do," the man said.

"Are they always part of the poverty group?" It was a shot in the dark, but it seemed like it would fit.

The man nodded. "Aye," he said. "They're usually here so you were probably right in your identification. Like all their type, if there's a chance to get summat for nought, they're first in line."

"You didn't see Harry here with them?"

The man shook his head. "But I only saw the dead man's photo in the paper. I wouldn't swear he wasn't here."

"I understand," Pauline said. "Now, I promised to sing a hymn with the ladies, so you must excuse me. Thank you for talking to me. I learned something new tonight."

"Hey," the man Pauline now knew as Alf said. "If you sing a song with those folks, you must sing one with us. Them's the rules."

"I didn't hear of any rules," Pauline said. "Anyway, I'm not from here. I only know Yorkshire songs."

"Then we'll do *On Ilkley Moor Ba Tat* and you can do the high bits," Alf said.

"Absolutely not," Pauline replied firmly. "That song goes on forever. I'd be here all night."

"Then *Bobby Shaftoe*," he said. "You must know that."

Pauline looked around at the eager faces and realized she couldn't refuse. They looked like puppies waiting to have a ball thrown for them.

"Very well," she said. "*Bobby Shaftoe* and no more."

The moment Alf had his group primed to start, Pauline could see Theresa was gathering her own group together. She sighed. People were the silliest creatures sometimes. Sadly, as she knew, sometimes they weren't.

After they'd wrapped up the song, Pauline thanked them once again for their help and made her escape before they could demand she take part in another. Like puppies, this was a game she would tire of long before they did.

"Miss Riddell," Theresa said, sternly, when she rejoined the women. "Your defection is a cruel blow to we few females. We demand two hymns in recompense."

Pauline laughed. "And if I do, those ruffians will demand I join them for another song. No. You each get my support for one song. I'll not play favorites. I may need their help sometime in the future and then where would I be?"

"Then what shall it be?" Theresa asked.

"It has to be something I know," Pauline replied.

"We have our hymn books," Theresa said, "and we can share."

Pauline thought. "Easter isn't so very far away. What about *There is a green hill far away*?"

While the group were leafing through their books to find the page, Pauline asked. "You aren't here all night, are you?"

Theresa smiled. "That would be more than even we could stand. No, the viewing hours end at seven-thirty, the Gospels leave by eight, and we leave after that. We're only here to persuade everyone who handles the book and comes to view the book to pressure their Member of Parliament into supporting our cause."

Pauline shook her head. "You want to turn the clock back five hundred years and Alf and his ruffians want to go back a thousand years. You should compromise at a date you can both support."

Theresa smiled. "A thousand years would suit us very nicely as well. After all, the monks who made the gospels book weren't your Church of England."

"Do any of the visitors respond to your protest?"

Pauline asked, avoiding a discussion she knew would last all night as it had for centuries.

Theresa shook her head. "Sadly, no. They scurry away as fast as they can." She smiled and continued, "But the seeds have been planted. Who knows which one will take root and maybe turn the tide? Now, everyone has the page so let's rouse them with *There is a green hill*."

After the hymn was sung, Pauline took her leave despite, once again, pleas for her to stay. It must get tedious, she thought looking at their eager expressions, protesting with the same faces and same message. A new face, such as hers, broke up the monotony. She was about to return to her car when she realized she hadn't yet viewed the book and, even though she knew it was a copy, she made her way into the cathedral where the line was down to the final stragglers.

Pauline bought a ticket at the small booth set up inside the door. The ticket seller seemed glad of the business. Pauline surmised most people had bought their tickets ahead of their visit and the poor woman was bored for most of her shift.

A roped path steered her through the doors and into the interior, which made her blink. Outside was darkness, inside was lit and even though it was subdued as befitted such a solemn place and viewing, it still felt bright to her eyes. The path took her through the nave, past the tomb of St. Cuthbert and eventually to stand in front of a solid looking, wheeled viewing case in which the book was opened at a page that began with a gloriously worked capital *I*. There were few people here now and she was able to spend time admiring the artistry of the script while wondering what the words said. Were they Latin or Old Anglo-Saxon? Were they both? There seemed to be more script between the lines. Either way, in their elaborately handwritten script, the words were indecipherable to her.

Pauline returned to her car musing on the effect of time on people, places, and ancient artifacts. History had never been her subject but with this case she had just a glimmering of what it meant to others and how passionately people could cling to their past. She hoped the real book was in the hands of someone with such a passion and not someone who just wanted money, no matter how noble they thought their cause was.

These thoughts stayed with her until she was home. Then she snapped back into action and called Inspector Ramsay. There was no answer.

Disappointed, she joined the Bertrams around the fire and tried to concentrate on her book, *Fahrenheit 451*. It was science fiction and Pauline didn't like science fiction but her boss, Dr. Enderby, did and he'd recommended it. She was tempted to just tell him she'd read it and hope he didn't ask her questions. At present, after days of reading and re-reading, all she could confidently say was it was about book-burning. Pauline liked censorship even less than she liked science fiction, but she heartily wished that, if there were going to be book burnings in the future, they'd start soon and use *Fahrenheit 451* as the kindling. Next time Dr. Enderby recommended a book, she'd ask Mr. Bertram to read it and give her the condensed version.

At bedtime, she tried Ramsay again and this time he was home. She explained about Gently and urged him to pass this on to the police in Durham, which he said he would.

"You didn't make yourself known to those men, did you?" Ramsay asked anxiously.

"Of course, I didn't. Though I will if you can't put a rocket up the local police's backsides, Inspector."

He laughed. "Miss Riddell," he said. "I'm shocked at such language from one so young and innocent."

"I'm being exposed to some pretty unsavory characters while in your company, Inspector. You have only yourself to blame if I go to the bad."

"I will do all in my power to get them moving, Miss Riddell," he replied. "You keep away from those men until there's been a positive development."

With that, Pauline had to be satisfied and she made her way upstairs in a lighter frame of mind. If these men were as violent as she'd heard, there'd be something to link them to Harry Common and his death. It was just a matter of time.

Chapter Twenty

THE KILLER ARRESTED

AS DR. ENDERBY entered the office next morning at work, he handed Pauline a national newspaper.

"You're in the news again, Pauline," he said, as he made his way past her desk into his office.

He'd opened the paper at the article she was mentioned in, and Pauline read it with a sinking stomach. Sooner or later, the police or her employer were going to tire of this notoriety she was gathering and cut her adrift.

The article suggested the government's denial of the missing Gospels was a smokescreen, and the amazing Miss Riddell was closing in on who had them. The rumors now were so loud, it couldn't be anything but true, the article claimed. This third article was worse than the previous two, Pauline thought. She was almost nauseous with a peculiar mix of fear and fury.

Pauline picked up the phone and dialed the Morpeth Herald office. Poppy didn't work there anymore, she was told. She'd moved on to greater things. Pauline put down the handset. Poppy was out of control and Pauline had no way of reining her in. Her stomach felt like it had hit the floor.

By evening, when Dr. Enderby's solemn silence throughout the day was making Pauline ever more afraid for her job, the phone rang. She jumped as if electrocuted.

"Dr. Enderby's office," she said as firmly as she could, but to her ears, she could hear the trembling in her own voice.

"It's me, Miss Riddell," Ramsay said. "I have good news."

"I could use some good news, Inspector. What is it?"

"The Durham police have picked up your friend, Gently, and he's confessed to hitting Harry Common."

"And why did he do that?" Pauline asked, excitement building.

"He says it was an altercation about a union matter. He says Common hit him first, which isn't true. Harry Common's hands showed no sign of a struggle, let alone a fight."

"If he sticks to this story, we'll get nowhere," Pauline said.

"As he well knows," Ramsay said. "Anyway, for now he's been charged with manslaughter, and he's being kept in custody."

"Is there evidence other than the mark from a ring?"

"No, but he hadn't thrown the rings away and our search found and matched them to the mark on Common's face."

"That should be enough for him," Pauline said. "Now we have a link between him, Harry, and the others. We must find one to the theft."

"Baby steps, Miss Riddell. Baby steps."

"We don't have time for baby steps," Pauline said. "We

need a giant leap. Now he's in custody, someone may be willing to talk."

"We may have that about to happen," Ramsay said. "The team thinks they've identified a man who called a few days ago demanding money for the safe return of the Gospels."

"That ransom strikes me as odd, Inspector," Pauline said. "Either the man really has the Gospels and that's how he knows they're missing or he's delusional."

"We hope it's the first," Ramsay said. "He keeps calling, even when the government denied they were missing so it's a strong delusion if he is deluded."

"I think the fact you keep answering his calls keeps him phoning," Pauline said. "It confirms his delusion."

"Possibly," Ramsay replied. "We'll know tomorrow one way or the other."

"Inspector," Pauline said, anxiously, "have you seen today's papers?"

"No. Why?"

"You may want to before you go back to the office," Pauline said. "Your Task Force leader won't be pleased."

"Another article by Poppy?"

"Yes. It's bad. She's now claiming there are rumors the government is deliberately hiding the truth about the Lind-isfarne Gospels and you and I are closing in on their whereabouts."

"Can't you get her to stop?" Ramsay asked. "This will cause real trouble. Governments don't like people being unpleasant about them, particularly when the person speaking is telling the truth. They have ways of taking revenge."

"You think Poppy may be in danger?"

"I think you, me, *and* Poppy, may be in danger. You must make her see sense," Ramsay said.

"I tried. She's left her flat without a forwarding address," Pauline said. "I suspect she's in London."

"I suspect her colleagues told her to go into hiding until the storm she's creating blows over," Ramsay said. "She may still be nearby."

Pauline laughed. "If I believed you about the government getting revenge, I'd follow her lead and go into hiding myself."

"Miss Riddell, are you a Gilbert and Sullivan fan?" Ramsay asked.

"No. Why?"

"In *Pirates of Penzance*, the pirate king sings the line, *many a king on a first-class throne, if he wants to call his crown his own, must somehow manage to get through, more dirty work than ever I do*," Ramsay said. "And that's true whether your government is a king or an elected official. Find her and stop her. For all our sakes."

"You can't really think we're in physical danger, Inspector," Pauline said, unsettled by the seriousness in his voice.

"Accidents happen," Ramsay said. "Jobs disappear, people disappear. Things happen all the time, Miss Riddell. This is trivial to you and me, but it isn't to someone in power who's being made to look ridiculous by it."

"I'll find her," Pauline said. "But if she's in hiding, it won't be easy."

Ramsay laughed. "Unlike Theresa Thompson, your friend Poppy isn't a trained agent. She'll have left a trail. If my boss is as angry as I think he's going to be, you should find Poppy before he does."

Pauline hung up the phone, trembling as she replaced the handset. She couldn't fully believe what Ramsay had said and yet, only weeks ago, two men who she'd exposed as spies were whisked out of the country in exchange for our spies being held abroad. If there'd been no one to exchange with, what would have happened to Wagner and Murdock?

Another restless night, planning how to find Poppy before the police did, left her exhausted by morning.

"You don't look well, dear," Mrs. Bertram said, watching Pauline pick at her breakfast.

"I'm fine," Pauline said crossly. She gave herself a mental shake, and continued, "Sorry, I didn't sleep well. I tried to find Poppy yesterday and she's gone. I must speak to her."

Mrs. Bertram said, "I'll talk to her mum this morning and set her on finding Poppy if she doesn't already know where she is."

"Thank you," Pauline said. "Maybe she moved back in with her parents."

Mr. Bertram gave a harsh laugh. "Unlikely," he said.

Mrs. Bertram explained, "Poppy and her parents had a falling out last year. They didn't approve of the life she was living and tried to persuade her against it. Poppy left home after a furious row and they haven't spoken since, so far as I know."

"Do what you can," Pauline said. "She's putting herself in danger with these new articles she's writing."

"I saw that one yesterday," Mr. Bertram said. "It was outrageous. A responsible editor wouldn't have published it but with the political situation what it is, I smell a rat. The paper is looking to change the government."

"But, dear," Mrs. Bertram said. "A missing book wouldn't be enough to do that."

Mr. Bertram said grimly, "This is a national treasure and there's a mystery on what happened to the book when it was taken off display for examination. If there's truth to Poppy's articles that will be construed as government incompetence. Alone, it can't change anything but drip, drip, drip these stories of incompetence into the public's mind, and well, the next election isn't so far away."

"It's madness," Pauline said, "and yet, I don't see any other explanation. Why would they continue to post Poppy's articles when they've been denied by the government, the church, the police, by everybody?"

"We'll find Poppy," Mrs. Bertram said, "and if her mother doesn't box her ears, I will!"

"That's the spirit," Mr. Bertram said, rising from the breakfast table. "Don't worry, Pauline. The unofficial union of mothers will find her for you quicker than even you could."

"I hope so," Pauline said, remembering what Ramsay had said about his Task Force leader.

Chapter Twenty-One

ANOTHER ONE CAUGHT

ONLY PARTLY RE-ASSURED by the promise she'd been given concerning the search for Poppy, Pauline went through her workday in a fog of feverish imaginings that flipped from Poppy to the man demanding money.

Who was it demanding money for the return of the Lindisfarne Gospels? Ramsay said the voice on the phone was not a cultured one so it wasn't Sir Robert or Sir Arthur, the most likely of the collectors; anyway, they would want to keep the book, not sell it back.

She hoped it wasn't a husband of one of the church ladies or one of the nutty nationalists; they'd all been too kind to this nosy young woman asking them awkward questions.

Would the police catch the caller? At the end of the workday, she left the offices quickly, drove to the nearest telephone box, and called Ramsay.

He laughed when he heard her voice. "You couldn't wait to hear it in the news, Miss Riddell?"

"Surely, it won't be in the news," Pauline replied,

"because the Gospels aren't missing."

"That's true. It will be interesting to see how my superiors and our press officer handle this one," he agreed.

"Did you catch them?"

"We did and it's no one we've seen before," Ramsay said. "It seems to be just a crank who took it into his head the Gospels really were missing. Poppy's articles helped him there, and he thought the authorities would pay up without making too much fuss to keep the secret."

"I don't believe there's no connection to our protesters, Inspector," Pauline said. "When we spoke the other day, you said the caller was 'rough sounding' not cultured. Doesn't that likely tie him in with the nationalists or that Temperley and his poverty group?"

"Maybe," Ramsay said. "We're still checking his background. He's a local man so he won't be hard to identify."

"He's not giving his real name, I take it, Inspector."

Ramsay laughed. "He says he's George Windsor. Unfortunately, he came prepared. There's nothing in his pockets to say who he really is. However, it's just a matter of circulating his photo to the local Durham bobbies on the beat and we'll have him.

"Well," Pauline replied. "I can't help but be disappointed, Inspector. I felt sure there'd be a clear connection, maybe even the key to this whole affair."

"It's early days, Miss Riddell," Ramsay replied. "We only got him into custody this afternoon. The link may appear soon, and all this will be over. Then you'll be even more disappointed."

Pauline considered for a moment. "Inspector, can I suggest a short cut. Bring a photo of this man and we'll go to the cathedral right now and show it to the church ladies.

They're there every night. If he's ever shown up as part of either of the two groups of men, they'll know."

"It would speed things up," he said, thoughtfully. "Very well. Shall we say the cathedral in one hour, Miss Riddell? Then you can introduce me to your friends."

Pauline made good time. She broke every speed limit between her workplace and Durham Cathedral to be on time. As she impatiently waited, a police car pulled up at the curb outside the gates and she saw Ramsay step out carrying a large envelope. She waved vigorously to catch his attention and he waved the envelope in reply.

"Theresa," Pauline said, as Ramsay joined them, "this is Inspector Ramsay. He has a photo he'd like you and the others to look at."

"What is it?" Theresa asked, as Ramsay slid the photo out of the envelope.

"It's a man we have in custody," Ramsay said, "and Miss Riddell felt he might be familiar to you or others in your group who've been protesting here these past days."

"Is this the man you think killed Harry Common, Inspector?" Theresa asked.

"No," Ramsay replied. "We're holding this man on an entirely different charge, but it is related to the same investigation."

Theresa called the women together and they studied the photo. In the evening darkness it wasn't easy to see, and the group moved over to the few lights around the open doorway.

"He was with the poverty group sometimes," a woman said.

"You're right, Ethel," another said. "Not every time but more than once."

"I know him," another said. "He's a wastrel. He lives on the same street as my Aunt Dot."

"Do you know his name?" Ramsay asked.

"Joe something," the woman replied, frowning. "Joe... Paisley. That's it, Joe Paisley."

Ramsay nodded. "And you're all sure you've seen him here."

"Very sure," the first woman said. "He was one of the more unpleasant of them at the beginning when they were calling us names."

"They did too, Inspector," Theresa said. "They really had a grudge against us and the nationalists over there." She gestured to the men across the lawn who were watching them with interest.

"Didn't like having competition, I expect," Ramsay said. "Is there anything else you can tell me about this man?"

The women shook their heads. "We don't really know him, Inspector," Theresa said. "Except as one of an unpleasant group of people, and what Elsie has told you."

"I'd like Elsie to tell me again what she knows of him and this time I'll take notes," Ramsay said, which he did, as Elsie spoke.

When he'd finished, Ramsay and Pauline made their way across the grounds to the waiting police car.

"This was a good idea of yours, Miss Riddell," Ramsay said. "Much quicker than looking up his family and friends and all the rest of it. We now know he is linked to a group who were protesting vigorously and have gone quiet since the Gospels went back on display. This man, Joe, might well be the genuine spokesman for the poverty group, if they *are* present holders of the loot."

"I'm sure of it, Inspector. Now we just have to prove it and find the book."

"And we'll both be back to humdrum everyday life," Ramsay said, smiling. "However, you should know, Joe, or George, is insisting he has the Gospels and the only way we'll get them from him is with a large cash sum and free passage out of the country."

"The worst of it is," Pauline said. "We can't be sure he doesn't have them. Someone does, why not him?"

"Unless he's part of a better organized gang, he doesn't have them. If they'd fallen from the sky on his head, he wouldn't know what hit him," Ramsay replied. "Still, he may know where they are, which is why we have to break him down and get him telling the truth."

"And I still must find evidence to link that man Gently to one or both of the robberies, Inspector," Pauline reminded him. "He's part of the same group of men who were almost certainly responsible for this in some way, and I want him put away for a long time. Mrs. Common deserves that much."

"Well, here are the photos you asked for," Ramsay said, handing over the envelope. "I hope you can link them there, too. It would wrap this up nicely, don't you think?"

"I do, and I also think it will, Inspector."

"I told you that talking to the women would pay dividends, Miss Riddell," Ramsay said, grinning. "You shouldn't be so quick to write women off as second division."

"I did no such thing!" Pauline cried.

"I remember you saying, quite clearly, 'I'm not sure I like this constant theme of I get to talk to the women, Inspector.' Or was that some other Miss Riddell?"

"You know very well I was concerned that *I* was being fobbed off on work no one else wanted to do," Pauline said. "Not that I thought the women had nothing useful to say."

He grinned. "My point remains. Whether you felt it was the women or you that were being slighted, which by the way, you weren't, you've achieved good results."

Pauline laughed. "I won't respond to your teasing anymore, Inspector. I bid you goodnight." She turned and walked away.

"Good night, and phone me tomorrow with what you find," he called after her.

"I'm not sure I shall now," Pauline called back, waving dismissively.

Chapter Twenty-Two

PAULINE PROPOSES A SOLUTION

PAULINE WALKED QUICKLY to the Wheatsheaf with the bundle of photos Ramsay had given her.

The woman serving studied the photos and said, pointing to a group of men in a police photo, "Those four are the ones who were talking to that man who was killed. I'm sure of it. They're in here often enough."

"Would you swear to it in court?" Pauline asked.

She laughed. "I not only wouldn't, I also wouldn't tell the police, even if they asked. I have to live here, you know."

As this was the answer Pauline had expected, she wasn't too disappointed. She was making progress, just not enough to link the men to any of the crimes, except for Harry's death, and it was still a moot point as to whether the police would follow through on the charges they'd laid against Gently. Yet the coincidence of Harry being in this place he never normally came to, the day after the thefts, was just too much.

"Which is the one who's always fighting?" Pauline asked, though she was sure she knew just by looking at the group. One was a particularly surly, hard-looking man. His stare into the camera gave her the shivers.

"That one," the barmaid said, pointing to the man Pauline had guessed.

"Are the others in the bar tonight?" Pauline asked.

The woman looked genuinely alarmed. "The others are, yes. You aren't thinking of approaching them, I hope?"

"As the thug is in custody right now, I might be safe," Pauline said. "You think they'd dislike a strange woman approaching them in the saloon bar?"

"I know they would, and you'd hear about it in very colorful language, I promise you," the barmaid said.

"I probably shouldn't wait for them to leave the pub then," Pauline said, laughing.

The woman looked at her incredulously. "Didn't you understand any of what I told you? The man who spoke to them that night is dead!"

"You said the violent one wasn't with them tonight," Pauline said. "Are you saying they're all violent?"

"I'm saying you keep away from them, all of them. We had three times the business in the pub before they moved in and made it their meeting place."

"People are scared of them?"

"People know what kind of people they are," the barmaid said. "That's enough to move to a safer local."

"That's interesting," Pauline said. "That they were known to be, let's say 'bad people' even before the death of Harry Common."

"Interesting to you, maybe. A nightmare to Mr. and Mrs. Jobson who own this pub and to us, their staff."

"Do people think they're criminals?" Pauline asked.

"Not that I know of," the barmaid said. "People just think they're thugs. They're enforcers for the metalworker's union and they collect money for the IRA."

"The Irish Republican Army?" Pauline asked. "Here, in the north-east of England."

"That's what the men say. They've never threatened or demanded money from me so I can't confirm that."

"Oh dear," Pauline said. "I thought the northern nationalists were nutty enough or the church ladies."

The barmaid was puzzled. "Northern nationalists? Church ladies?"

"They're two groups protesting up at the cathedral," Pauline said. "I asked them if they'd seen Harry Common when I thought he might have ties to those men through there, after all he was a metalworker."

"I've never heard of local nationalists," the barmaid said, "but them Catholic church women may well have a link. The local Catholic church priest is Irish. Mind, I don't say he's a member of the IRA, but it wouldn't be impossible, would it?"

"No, it wouldn't," Pauline said thoughtfully. It wasn't unusual for Catholic priests to be Irish, of course. In fact, it was common, but here was a strange potential link that no one else in the investigation had noticed. Should she follow that trail?

"Well," she said, at last, "I'll take your advice and leave before the men do. That way I shan't bump into them."

She took her sherry to a small table and scribbled notes in her book as she sipped her drink. When she was finished, she returned to the bar and stood where she could see through into the saloon. The men were still there. She handed the glass to the barmaid. "I'm going now. They seem set for the night."

Outside, she considered her next move. It was late. The cathedral doors would be closing soon, and the protesters would be leaving. Was it worth interviewing them again tonight?

In the end, she decided to try. A brisk walk took her to the cathedral, and she was pleased to see the protesters still milling aimlessly about. They'd trampled the afternoon snow to a slushy mess. Most had rubber boots on, Pauline noted, so they'd come prepared.

"Hello again, Theresa," Pauline said, smiling. "Can I ask one very quick question?"

"Of course," Theresa said, handing her sign to one of the other women and following Pauline to stand a little way off from the others. "What is it?"

"This is going to sound odd," Pauline said, "but I wondered, is your local priest Irish?"

"He is, yes. Why?"

"I wondered if his feelings about the Reformation were as radical as yours?"

Theresa laughed. "It's called the *English* Reformation, Pauline. If you recall your history lessons, the Irish rightly declined to get caught up in such arrant nonsense."

"Still, it has caused such a great divide between our two peoples," Pauline said. "I just wondered."

"Father O' Reilly does everything he can to dissuade us from our present course, Pauline. I promise you. He doesn't want any trouble in his parish. And certainly not of the political kind."

"You've set my mind at rest," Pauline said. "These peculiar links and the ideas that spring from them pop up all the time when you set out to investigate even the simplest thing."

"But none of it has anything to do with us here in the Cathedral Precinct," Theresa said.

"You think not, but I now know the man whose death I'm investigating was talking to some of the poverty action group on the night he died so, you see, there are links."

"They've not been here much the last two nights," Theresa said, "as we said when you were here earlier."

"Some of them are in a nice warm pub right now not so far from here. They may be coming here for the last few minutes as the doors close."

Theresa shook her head. "Not them. The rush is over. There's hardly anyone here when the doors close. I think we're safe from their impertinence tonight."

"Are they really unpleasant to you?"

Theresa shook her head. "They're rude, crude, and sarcastic but the policeman is always here so it never amounts to more than that."

"The barmaid didn't like them either," Pauline said. "But being unlikeable doesn't make you a criminal. I sometimes wish it did." She smiled to show she was joking.

Theresa laughed. "We'd all be in jail at some time, if it were, Pauline. Be careful what you wish for."

"It's true," Pauline said. "I'm often less than my best to people at work or during investigations. I heard you were in the Special Operations Executive during the war, Theresa. That must have been exciting."

"Oh, not so much," Theresa said. "I was mainly training people. I speak French and, although we only hired people who were already fluent in French, I was assigned to work with them. Try to trip them into saying the wrong thing. That sort of thing. More like a schoolmistress than a spy."

"I'm still impressed," Pauline said, laughing. She noted Theresa's description of her role was considerably less exciting than the one Ramsay had described. Probably she was bound by the Official Secrets Act, but could it be more? Hiding her true capabilities from a nosy investigator, for instance? Would a wartime spy have knowledge of IRA operatives?

Pauline drove back to the Bertrams' house with her mind full of the new information she'd uncovered. Could the IRA have stolen the Gospels? They were an essentially left-wing political group, but all their members were from Catholic backgrounds and the Gospels were said to have a lot of influences from the Irish church missionaries of that day. Maybe the theft was originally for money to fund their usual campaigns of sabotage but maybe it had the extra bonus of embarrassing the British establishment? Pauline decided Ramsay was right to hate politics and politicians.

Overnight, Pauline spent time thinking the case through and woke the next morning with a headache and the determination of an unpleasant duty she must do. Before even sitting down to the cooked breakfast Mrs. Bertram was preparing, Pauline phoned Inspector Ramsay.

"You're early today, Miss Riddell," he said. "I don't think you've ever called before breakfast."

"I've spent the whole night tossing and turning," Pauline said, "and I thought it best to tell you why. I'll let you decide if it's relevant or not."

"I'm sure it will be," Ramsay said, "or it wouldn't have given you such bother."

"It's kind of you to say so, Inspector. Anyway, two things are bothering me. They're both speculative and I'm not sure how your Task Force might react if you don't share them carefully."

"They'll behave as they see fit," Ramsay said. "We can only give them what we know and hope for the best."

"I hate doing this because I like the people involved," Pauline said.

"I understand but I repeat, we can only tell people what we think, and they must use their own discretion."

"All right," Pauline said. "First, I've learned some of the poverty group people raise money for the Irish Republican Army."

"It happens more than you think, Miss Riddell," Ramsay said. "They have a lot of sympathizers, particularly among the more leftish political activists."

"And the Catholic women's church has an Irish priest," Pauline said. "Could they want the Gospels for funds and for the propaganda coup?"

Ramsay paused. "It's not an unrealistic idea," he said slowly, "but I'm not convinced."

"Nor am I," Pauline admitted. "I just saw a possible connection to a group who could have carried out these robberies and had a motive to do so."

"There are many Irish priests," Ramsay said, thoughtfully, "and many people who collect money for the IRA and other groups in our cities. Is your suspicion enough to round up and interrogate honest women and a priest? I'll give it to the Task Force leader and let him decide."

"Here's my second thought, Inspector," Pauline said. "We know Harry Common was involved in some way with the poverty group, and we know he is linked with Sir Robert Lauriston, who is a great collector of antiquities and who has made no secret of his desire to own the Gospels, though not just for himself."

"You think Sir Robert has them?"

"I don't know," Pauline said, unhappily. "I hope not. I really like him. I'm just pointing out a series of connections that I've found during my research."

"He's a well-liked, well-respected man," Ramsay said. "I've never heard a word spoken against him. How do you think this went?"

"I think Temperley, the leader of the poverty group, how I hate calling them that, commissioned Harry to make a replacement for the attaché case the Gospels were transported in. That way they could switch the two cases to gain time for their escape. Harry made a case but told Sir Robert what was happening. Sir Robert quickly realized he could capitalize on their plan – I can see him smiling at the double-cross he planned – and asked Harry to make a second matching case."

"But how did they make the switch?"

"I don't know exactly," Pauline admitted. "I'm guessing that they got into the bank first and made the exchange. Then the robbers got in and took the case, which must have been weighted to seem like the book was in it. Or maybe it was Harry who was assigned to steal the Gospels and handed the case over to the group. I don't really know how it went but I'm sure Sir Robert has it."

"You think Harry gave Sir Robert the case with the Gospels in it and Sir Robert is hiding it until the search died down?" Ramsay asked.

"Exactly," Pauline said. "Unfortunately for Harry, the robbers opened the case he'd given them and discovered the fraud. Probably Harry and Sir Robert thought the thieves would have left the case and its locks intact because they weren't interested in it themselves."

"When they discovered the double-cross, they lured

Harry to Durham where they planned to beat out of him where the Gospels were, but Harry died?"

"That's what I think! I don't know if it's enough, Inspector," Pauline said. "But you should search Sir Robert's house if you can."

"None of that is enough to get a search warrant, Miss Riddell," Ramsay said. "It's the same with your priest and Catholic ladies. However, the London officers may have influence that I don't. We'll see."

Chapter Twenty-Three

FIND POPPY!

RAMSAY WASN'T SURPRISED to once again find himself intercepted as he entered the Durham Headquarters Building and was taken to a private office. This time, both the Task Force leader and the Chief Commissioner were in attendance. Neither of them spoke until the two officers who'd escorted Ramsay had left the room.

"I thought I'd made the position clear last time we spoke," the Task Force leader said, his expression murderous.

"I assume we're talking about that journalist's articles," Ramsay said.

"You know damn well we are," the Task Force leader said. "There was another one yesterday and it's making some very important people angry."

"I can't be responsible for what's printed in the press," Ramsay said.

The Chief Commissioner said, "And yet she says you and that other woman are closing in on the book's location,

157

Ramsay. How does she know this if you aren't feeding her the story?"

"I'm not even speaking to her, let alone feeding her the story," Ramsay replied. "I haven't spoken to her since the moment I joined this team."

"She's doing all this why?" the Task Force leader asked.

"Because I told her I wasn't working on anything important, and I wouldn't be sharing anything with her. After her part in the two cases Miss Riddell was involved in, she'd grown used to being part of things. Now she feels rejected, I guess," Ramsay said.

"She's wrecking your career, Ramsay," the Task Force leader said. "I'm not going to let her wreck mine."

"Now, Superintendent," the Commissioner said, severely. "That sounds like a threat."

"It does to me too, sir," Ramsay added.

"I simply meant I won't have her ruining this investigation and preventing our successful conclusion of it," the Task Force leader said.

Turning and speaking to the Commissioner, he said, "I'm sorry if you misunderstood me, sir." His expression directed at Ramsay, when he turned back to him, was less conciliatory.

"Ramsay," the Commissioner said. "You need to find this reporter and smooth things between you. Her pique at being kept at arm's length can't be allowed to jeopardize this investigation."

"Unfortunately, she's left her apartment, sir, without leaving a forwarding address. We haven't yet found her new location."

"But you are looking?" the Commissioner asked.

"Her friend, Miss Riddell, is looking," Ramsay said. "She can't have gone far."

"I suggest you join the search, Inspector," the Task Force leader said. "You're the one who knows her; you're the one who created the problem by letting her have too much access on the earlier investigations. Your problem has become ours, so you'd better fix it and fast."

"Very well, sir," Ramsay said. "Before I go, I have two suggestions you might like to consider."

"They'd better be good."

"I leave it to you to decide if they're good," Ramsay said. "I would do more on them myself, but they're outside the orders I've been given."

"So, you do remember those," the Task Force leader said. "I'm pleased to hear it. Well, what are these suggestions?"

Ramsay told him briefly what Pauline had told him.

The Task Force leader nodded. "Sounds like rubbish to me, but we'll check them out. Now you find that reporter."

Ramsay returned to his desk in the Task Force office, raging inside. He called the Morpeth Herald where he was told, as Pauline had been, they didn't know where Poppy was. Ramsay demanded to be put through to the proprietor and made it known the Herald was in great danger of losing the confidence of the police. It took a few minutes of insincere assurances of the Herald's honest intentions before Ramsay got the reply he wanted. They would find Poppy and let her know the police wanted to speak to her.

He phoned Pauline at her work. She told him of Mrs. Bertram's promise to find her niece.

"Would it help if I called Poppy's parents?" Ramsay asked.

"Not yet," Pauline said. "They may have fallen out with their daughter but may rally around her as a family if there was a semblance of a threat."

"You don't know of anyone, a girlfriend or a young man perhaps, she might be staying with?"

Pauline remembered the man with Poppy on New Year's Eve. "I don't know of any steady boyfriend," she said, at last. "Someone might."

"Not her parents by what you've told me," Ramsay said. "Work colleagues, perhaps?"

"I'll try them, Inspector," Pauline said. "Again, I don't think a heavy police presence is a help in this case."

Ramsay laughed. "A heavy police presence isn't often a help, Miss Riddell, but we still have to do it. But I take your point. See what you can get out of them first."

He rang off and considered his next steps. He could continue investigating the bank robbery or he could find Poppy. The bank robbery was important to the Gospels investigation, the possible recovery of a national treasure, the well-being of the robbed bank and its insurance company, and the public at large who would be safer with hardened criminals behind bars. Finding Poppy on the other hand might save his future life. It was no contest really. He'd best find that damned reporter.

Pauline returned home from work to eat a quick evening meal. As they ate, she asked Mrs. Bertram if there was any news about Poppy.

"Not yet, dear," Mrs. Bertram replied. "She's not with her parents nor with any of the families she's friends with. That we *do* know."

"None of them had any knowledge of where she might be?"

"They say not," Mrs. Bertram replied, "but you know how young people are. They have such misplaced loyalties."

Ignoring this aspersion on her age group, Pauline asked where the mothers would try next.

"Not all Poppy's family and friends are on the tele-phone," Mrs. Bertram replied. "Tomorrow we'll visit those who aren't. We should have them all contacted by tomorrow night. Can't the police help, Pauline? She is a missing person, after all."

"Strictly speaking," Pauline said, "she isn't a missing person. She's an adult who has left her current address and that's all we know. She is most likely in London now that she's getting articles published in papers down there. It would be the logical thing for her to do."

"And we know it's what she's always wanted," Mr. Bertram said, interjecting for the first time. "I think that's where you'll find her."

"Only we won't find her if that's where she is," Pauline said. "London is too big. She could be hiding anywhere there, and we'd never find her."

"What are you going to do, Pauline?" Mr. Bertram asked.

"I'm going to visit the pubs in Morpeth tonight and hope someone knows something."

"It might be better if I or Mrs. Bertram came with you," he replied.

Pauline thanked him but declined the offer, pointing out young people would more likely give another young person, like her, information they wouldn't give parent-like people. Mr. Bertram nodded and went back to his meal. After they finished eating, Pauline dressed for a winter night walking between pubs.

She remembered Poppy had been a regular at the Black Bull and began there. The bar staff knew Poppy but weren't aware she was missing and had no idea where she might be. The few customers in the saloon seemed not to know Poppy at all, which Pauline thought suspicious but had to accept.

She set out to visit every pub on the main street and by ten o'clock had visited them all without any success. As she had to pass the Black Bull to get to her car, she called in there again.

It was much busier than when she'd been there earlier, with tables of younger people throughout the different rooms. Feeling it best simply to ask if anyone had seen Poppy that night, her being a friend and almost relation, Pauline began making her way around the tables. Just when she was about to give up in disgust, a bearded man that Pauline thought might have been Poppy's boyfriend at New Year said, "She moved to Newcastle with her boyfriend."

"She didn't tell me," Pauline said, pretending outrage at her friend's neglect. "It must be a recent move, or I'd have heard."

"Aye," the man replied. "It was last Saturday."

One of the girls at the table laughed. "When she told me she was going places, I thought she meant London, not Newcastle."

"You don't have an address or a phone number for her, do you?" Pauline opened the question out to the whole table. "Or the boyfriend's name?"

They shook their heads.

"Oh, well," Pauline said. "I'll just have to wait until she gets in touch. I'll give her a piece of my mind when she does. I've got something she needs to hear and the sooner the better."

Even this inducement didn't draw out any more information. Pauline thanked them and set out for home, where Mrs. Bertram pounced on her the moment she was in the door.

"Well," she said. "Did you learn anything?"

"I'm told she moved to Newcastle last weekend, but nobody claims to know exactly where."

Mrs. Bertram turned to her husband. "You work there. Can you find out where she might be?"

"I work there, dear," he replied placidly. "That's all I do in the city." He turned to Pauline and asked, "Is she alone?"

"I'm told she moved with her boyfriend," Pauline replied. "Nobody claims to know him, either."

"Not a lot to go on," Mr. Bertram said. "If the mothers can't give us anything tomorrow, a private detective or the police might have better luck."

Pauline nodded. "I want to find her before the police do. Her articles are causing them a lot of unpleasantness from above."

"I can imagine," Mr. Bertram said. "Then it's up to you and the league of mothers, Mrs. Bertram, to come to the rescue."

"They wouldn't actually harm her, would they?" Mrs. Bertram asked. "The police, I mean."

Pauline smiled encouragingly. "This is England and I'm sure they won't. But they won't mince words when they speak to her."

"Oh dear, what if we can't find her?"

"It will be a good learning experience for her, dear," Mr. Bertram said. "I warned you it might come to this. Poppy was never going to be content writing stories about minor events for the local paper. I know it's fashionable to want to be at the top of things, but young people rarely understand it comes with a lot of unpleasantness."

"I hoped she'd meet a nice young man and settle down," Mrs. Bertram said unhappily. She smiled wanly at Pauline. "It seems dull to you, I'm sure, but everyday ordinary life is usually the best."

Pauline laughed. "You can't expect me to agree. I'm still young."

Mrs. Bertram nodded. "And the future looks so far away but it comes on you faster than you think, dear. One day, you realize it's too late." She smiled and added, "You don't understand what I'm talking about and how could you. I'll try and explain it better. There are stages in life and if you miss one, it's gone. It can't be recovered. Remember that. Now, I'll make us all some Ovaltine to help us sleep."

Chapter Twenty-Four

PAULINE GOT IT WRONG

NEXT MORNING, Pauline called Ramsay and told him of her new information.

"Newcastle, you say," Ramsay said. "I'll ask DS Morrison, my old assistant, if he can find her. He has a new inspector as his boss right now, but I think he'll do it for me."

"He has to be discreet, Inspector," Pauline said. "If the Task Force hears he's searching for her without their knowledge, they'll be even more angry."

"I'm supposed to be looking for her, too," Ramsay said, "so I can say he's working for me. I just want us to speak to her first."

"Me too," Pauline said with feeling. "I don't like the sound of your London colleagues."

"They work in a more dangerous city," Ramsay said. "It makes them harder than we country boys."

Pauline laughed. "I can't imagine you as a country boy, Inspector."

"Perhaps not quite country," he agreed. "By the way, I

have some good news. Our London colleagues *do* have more pull than we country boys. Last night, we got a warrant to search your Catholic ladies' homes and the priest's and we pulled them in for questioning first thing this morning. Mid-morning, we got a warrant to search the poverty group leaders' homes and Sir Robert's fine mansion. It normally would take days to get these, even with more evidence. What do you think of that?"

"I think I begin to see where your cynicism comes from, Inspector," Pauline said. "I only hope you find something. It will raise you up in their estimation if it does."

"And the reverse is also true if they don't," Ramsay said with a humorless laugh. "It's the waiting to see which is my fate that keeps me in this job."

"When will you know?"

"The poverty people's homes are small, terraced houses so they'll be done by this afternoon. Sir Robert's place is huge. I think it will be much later."

"Will you phone me and tell me how it went?" Pauline asked.

"I certainly will, Miss Riddell," Ramsay said. "Particularly if only to spread the blame more widely."

Pauline smiled. She could imagine the wry expression on his face. "You're too kind, Inspector. And if there's credit to be shared?"

"None of it will reach me, let alone you, Miss Riddell. A woman of your age should know that by now."

"Till tonight then," Pauline said, and hung up the phone.

By evening, everyone was exhausted and depressed. For Mrs. Bertram it had been a fruitless day searching for Poppy, leaving her was very low in spirits. Pauline wasn't sure she didn't prefer the quieter Mrs. Bertram but felt genuinely sorry for her.

Mr. Bertram had spoken to private detectives in a bid to estimate how easily they thought it would be to find Poppy. Their replies hadn't encouraged him to hire one.

Pauline had wandered the streets of Newcastle after church, hoping to see Poppy, and showing a photo of her to everyone who would stop to look. By late afternoon, cold, wet, and footsore, she'd returned home in despair.

Consequently, their evening meal was eaten in depressed silence and the dishes washed and put away without the usual exchange of details from each other's days.

The noise of the phone ringing, for the first time was a happy sound to Pauline. Even better, for a moment, when she learned it was Inspector Ramsay.

"Can we meet, Miss Riddell?" he asked when Pauline took the phone from Mrs. Bertram.

"Not good news, then," Pauline said, her momentarily raised hopes dashed. "I'm sorry."

"Our usual place?" he asked. "In one hour?"

They met as they finished parking their cars at the back of the pub and walked in together. While Ramsay bought the drinks, Pauline found them a small table somewhat set off from the others, against a window. As it was Sunday, the ladies lounge wasn't busy, and she felt they could talk privately.

Ramsay arrived with their drinks, his face serious, drawn with tension. She guessed he'd had a rough final hour at work.

"Tell me the worst," Pauline said, raising her sherry glass and taking a good mouthful. Sometimes, sipping wouldn't do.

Ramsay walked her though the day's events and when

he'd finished explaining what the police had found and why they were now convinced neither the poverty group nor Sir Robert were in any way connected to the theft of the Gospels, or even the death of Harry Common, Pauline nodded disconsolately. She felt, and looked, deflated.

"And the Catholic ladies?" Pauline asked, hardly daring to hope this might be good news.

"Nothing," Ramsay said. "And now the Chief Constable is angry at us because of all the flak he's getting from these good people."

"I'm not helping on this case at all, am I?" Pauline asked. "I'm out of my depth here, with plots and politics, robberies and accidental deaths. I was lucky on those other two cases. I see that now."

"We can't always be right, Miss Riddell," Ramsay said in a bid to cheer her up. "They were reasonable suggestions. If either had been right, my superiors would be handing out medals to each other."

Pauline couldn't smile even at his usual sarcasm. "I think I let my experience of union men cloud my judgment, Inspector. Whenever they visit the plant, I'm often called upon to escort them to conference rooms and take minutes of the meetings. I find them intimidating. Their grim expressions and their harsh manners are chilling."

"You, who've faced down murderers, find working people frightening? I don't believe it."

"I don't find working people frightening," Pauline replied. "I find the people who claim to represent them intimidating."

"The workers vote for them, Miss Riddell."

Pauline laughed. There was no mirth in the sound. "They vote in public where everyone can see which way they voted. I said 'claim to represent them' for good reasons,

Inspector. Few of those representatives have truly been working men or would win in a secret ballot."

Ramsay nodded. "I agree. I know a lot about those folks through my line of work."

"The thing is, I agree with them that we need a fairer distribution of the benefits from our labors," Pauline said. "I just feel there must be a better way of getting it than the methods they employ. Those people will destroy the goose that lays the golden eggs, you mark my words."

Ramsay laughed. "A social reformer and a fighter for justice, Miss Riddell. You have your work cut out on the road ahead. I should warn you, one of the deepest divisions I see in our society is simply the public's taste. They will spend a fortune on toys and trinkets and fight any attempt to pay more for things they need, like clothes, food, shelter, and tools to make their lives better. Your two crusades come under the latter, I'm afraid. You'll never get your just desserts – if I may phrase it that way."

Pauline laughed. "I don't care for fancy desserts, Inspector. I'm a simple soul who prefers homecooked pastries and puddings, so maybe I'll get all I need."

"That's as much as we should expect from life," Ramsay said. "Now, if it wasn't those people, who was it? It brings it back to the Northumbrian nationalists for me."

"I'm not so sure," Pauline replied. "I hate to say this because I like Mrs. Thompson, but she isn't a dotty middle-aged widow. As you told me, she was an agent in the Intelligence Services in the war and not the sleeper kind of agent. She is fully trained in explosives and any number of dirty tricks. I still think there is something there, though it may not include the IRA."

"Even though that's true," Ramsay said, "the rest of her group weren't. I don't see how they could have done it."

"Easy," Pauline said. "The bank manager is a long-time friend. She told me that herself. More than that, he's a widower and she's a widow. It would be easy for her to manipulate him into wrongdoing if the circumstances were right."

"Miss Riddell," Ramsay said. "Do you have any reason to believe this or is this a fairy tale of your own making?"

"At present," Pauline said chillingly, "it's an avenue of enquiry I plan to pursue, Inspector. Not a *fairy tale*."

He laughed. "Your reproof is noted, Miss Riddell," he said. "I look forward to hearing what you find."

"I'm not sure I'll tell you now," Pauline said, smiling. "What line of fairy tale will you be following?"

"Still the bank robbery," Ramsay said. "And we know that isn't a figment of anyone's imagination, so there."

"Could the people who stole the Gospels really have organized a bank robbery at the same time?" Pauline asked. "It sounds far-fetched to me."

"Not as unlikely as two bank robberies in one city on the same night," Ramsay said. "That's a coincidence too far, even for your imagination."

"But they're different kinds of people," Pauline said. "One was violent and about cash and the other was peaceful and about a beautiful book."

"As I recall reading," Ramsay reminded her, "the present cover of the book was made in the 1700s because its original cover was torn off for its likely value centuries before, probably by Viking raiders. It doesn't follow that because the robberies appear to be a different class of people, that they in fact were. Money is money, whatever shape it comes in."

"I suppose," Pauline said. "Maybe my prejudice is at

play there, too. Intelligent, even cultured, people can be violent. Theresa Thompson, for example."

Ramsay nodded. "Brute force and ignorance will usually overcome all obstacles if they're intelligently applied."

"If you're right," Pauline said, "then our independent research should find a link between the church ladies and your Newcastle bank robbers. It would be a satisfying conclusion, though as I said, I hope not. I don't like it when I sympathize with the people I'm hunting. It makes me doubt."

"Then let's hope it isn't so," Ramsay said. "Let us hope Mrs. Thompson has put her violent training behind her and now lives a blameless life while our criminals are responsible for both thefts."

"Yes," Pauline said, lifting her sherry glass. "I'll toast to that." She sipped and then stopped. A horrible thought, a memory, had come to mind. "Inspector, did your people search Sir Robert's castle?"

"We searched his house and the outbuildings," Ramsay said. "Is that what you mean?"

Pauline shook her head. "When I visited his house, he joked about having the remains of a castle on the grounds. I didn't see it but I'm sure he didn't mean the present house."

"And you think the Gospels may be there?"

"It occurs to me a lot of things might be there. Things he doesn't show his regular visitors."

Ramsay looked at his watch. "If it was, it will be gone by now. We left the property over two hours ago. We surprised him when we arrived, but he wouldn't leave the Gospels on his property now, would he."

"He might," Pauline said. "If you didn't find it, why would you return?"

"We would have to get a new search warrant," Ramsay mused.

"It's a dry night," Pauline said. "A good night to be out getting some air."

"Trespassing is against the law, Miss Riddell," Ramsay said.

"Then you go home to bed," Pauline replied. "I feel the need for fresh air to clear my head."

Chapter Twenty-Five

A DEAD END AND A NEW HOPE

AS PAULINE SAID, it was a dry, frosty night and the moon and stars shone brightly enough to light their way across the meadow of frost-covered grass to the low, outer walls of the ruin. Pauline squatted down behind the remains of what must once have been the gatehouse of the small castle that protected the local lord, his family and tenants against Scottish raiders. She switched on her small flashlight and studied the outline of the ruin on her ordinance survey map.

"This map isn't very useful," she said disgustedly. It showed only a small square with some outer ruined walls.

"It showed us where to find the place," Ramsay said, surveying the ruins in the pale light. "If there is any room or cellar left that's useable, it must be over there under the keep." He pointed at an inner mound of earth with a single stone battlemented wall towering over it. There were no signs of a door.

They made their way to the mound and circled it. There was no door.

"Maybe there's a hatch on top of the mound," Pauline

said ascending the slope to the summit, which was only about a yard higher than the surrounding land. They slowly made their way across the top, brushing the frosty grass aside with their boots, hoping for a trapdoor hidden underneath. There was none.

"We should walk all around the remains of the outer walls," Ramsay said. "There may be a small room inside them."

They slid their way down and, one on each side of the low stone wall, walked the full circuit of the ruin.

"Nothing," Pauline said, in disgust. "If he ever had the Gospels, he's put it in a safer place than his house and grounds."

"I imagine he knew that when the Gospels were discovered to be missing, he would be among the first to be suspected and acted accordingly."

"We should get home," Pauline said, "before we're caught by his gamekeeper."

When they returned to their cars, Ramsay said, "I'm glad we did this. To have persuaded the Task Force to return and find nothing again would have destroyed what little credibility I have left among them."

"I'm worried my credibility among the Catholic ladies might be gone too if they guess I had anything to do with them being searched and interrogated," Pauline said miserably.

Ramsay laughed. "I don't think you should concern yourself about that. They weren't in the least put out. I think Mrs. Thompson, for one, enjoyed the interview."

"Still, I feel guilty leading you down three dead ends in one day, Inspector," Pauline said. "I hope nothing ill comes of it."

"It will blow over, Miss Riddell," Ramsay said. "Good night and happier hunting tomorrow."

The following evening, after work, Pauline returned to the cathedral where she found Theresa Thompson wasn't with the others. She asked after Theresa and was told Theresa had a cold.

"I knew standing out here night after night in all weathers couldn't be good for one's health," Pauline said to a chorus of objections that centered around the virtues of fresh, clean air and plenty of walking. The strengthening of the human spirit made an appearance too.

Pauline laughed. "My apologies," she said. "I hope Theresa will be better soon. Please give her my best wishes when you see her."

"She'll be sorry she missed you," one of the women said. "She enjoys your chats."

"I'm glad," Pauline said. "I certainly enjoy talking with her. She's a fascinating woman."

There was a chorus of agreement, which confirmed in Pauline's mind that Theresa was indeed the leader here, and one strong enough to inspire others beyond their own daily lives.

"Did you know she was in the Special Operations Executive in the war?" a woman asked.

"Was she?" Pauline asked, as though she didn't already know that.

"She was," the woman said. "She parachuted into France more than once and worked with the Resistance, sabotaging things," she ended lamely. The realization of what those 'things' implied was too much to confidently state.

"Then I'm surprised she should take such a pedestrian manner of bringing about change," Pauline said, smiling. "I should have thought a grand theft would have been well within her powers."

There was general agreement at this, before the woman said, "Theresa says to have a lasting solution, it must be a peaceful one. What you take by force, you can never hope to keep."

"Perhaps she's right," Pauline said. "Though you're attempting to recover what Henry VIII took by force four hundred and fifty years ago which would seem to weaken your argument."

"Our church is almost two thousand years old," the woman said. "Four hundred and fifty years isn't a lot compared to that."

"The police thought the poverty campaigners were plotting to steal the Gospels," Pauline said, throwing the blame on the police without a qualm of conscience. "Did you hear anything that might support that?"

The women shook their heads, and the spokeswoman said, "They wouldn't say anything when we were nearby anyway. They seemed to have a special dislike of us. Wrong class and wrong sex, I think."

Pauline laughed. "That's how I felt when I talked to them as well."

"To be fair," another woman added, "they didn't like the other group either. There were often times I thought they would start fighting. I'm glad they're gone, to be honest. I didn't like them, and I don't believe they cared about poverty at all." Again, there was a general murmuring of agreement.

"Perhaps it was the cover for a robbery," Pauline suggested.

"Wouldn't they be more agreeable if that were the

case?" the spokeswoman said. "More eager for friends and allies?"

"I don't know," Pauline replied. "To be honest, I only got involved because a mother wanted to know why her son had died. I'd had success in that sort of crime, you see. These shifting political currents and bank robberies aren't something I have any experience in at all."

"Do you think the man who died was involved?" the spokeswoman asked.

"He came to Durham and went to a pub he'd never been in, where he talked to a group of men who I now know were part of the poverty protesters. One of them followed him outside and struck him," Pauline said. "The coincidence of that happening just after the bank robbery may be just that, a coincidence. I feel there's more, which is why you find me here again tonight."

"I feel sorry for his mother," the spokeswoman said. "I read she's a widow. First her husband, and now her son is dead. I wish I could help but I can't think of anything that connects him with the poverty group that were here."

"They may be back soon," Pauline said. "The police have ruled out any connection between most of them and Harry Common's death and there's no evidence they were planning to steal the Gospels."

This was not a welcome suggestion, as she could see from the gloomy expressions of the group.

"You said rumors of a theft, Miss Riddell," a woman said. "We heard lots of joking about it, but I wouldn't call those rumors. Was there something more serious?"

"I'm not in the police's confidence," Pauline said, "but I understand there was talk in the wider community, art dealers and the like. And the press wrote articles about it."

"I hope that doesn't prevent the Gospels or any other treasure from being displayed in other parts of the country," the spokeswoman said. "We need more of these events, not less."

"I agree," Pauline said. "But I can see there may be a reluctance to let them go; at least in the near future when people as capable as Theresa are still young enough and active enough to carry out a theft. There must be many such people who are finding peacetime too dull to be bearable."

"Well Theresa isn't one of them," the spokeswoman said, firmly. "She often remarks how good it is to live without fear. Her wartime experiences cured her of that kind of excitement."

"I'm glad to hear it," Pauline said. "But the nationalists over there will have all done military training and so will many of the poverty group. Can we be sure one of them doesn't have similar skills and a hankering after excitement?"

"You'll have to ask them," the woman said.

"I shall," Pauline replied. "Alf over there will be tired of my prying but if there's a link to Harry Common's death, I need to find it."

She made her way over to the other group, where her usual contact, Alf, smiled wryly in greeting. "Miss Riddell, good evening. I warn you; I'm beginning to think you desire me for more than my knowledge; you're here so often."

Pauline smiled. "Good evening, Alf. I promise your virtue is safe from me. I really do visit only for information."

There was a chorus of derision at Alf's expense, which he waved aside imperiously. "Ignore these peasants, Miss Riddell. They're just jealous that I get all the attention. What can I help you with tonight?"

"I wondered about everyone's military service," Pauline

178

said. "I learned recently that Mrs. Thompson, the leader of your singing rivals across the way, was in the SOE during the war, which made me wonder about everything that's gone on in Durham these past days."

"You got me," Alf said. "I cannot tell a lie. I was in the commandoes and learned all the arts of bank robbing, unarmed combat skills, and how to hide in full sight from pursuers."

There was general laughter from the group, before someone said, "He was in an office at Acklington airfield, and his only training is in arithmetic."

"Now who do I believe, Alf?" Pauline said. "Your confession or this rumor?"

"I have to confess I may have exaggerated my wartime exploits to win your affection, Miss Riddell," Alf replied, grinning. "I think you'll also find the others here, who are so contemptuous of my war record, were equally safe at home when the war happened. We're none of us more than also-rans in the hero race."

"None of you are safecrackers, I suppose?"

Alf looked puzzled for a moment. Then he said, "Oh! You mean the bank robbery at the other side of town. Only Gerry could have done that. He works in a quarry, and they have explosives."

Gerry laughed. "He's right, Miss. I do work in the offices at a quarry. I even keep the records of how much explosive we have. You wouldn't want me to blow up anything with them, though. I wouldn't know which end to light."

"None of your quarry's explosives went missing, I suppose?" Pauline asked.

"Not ours, no. A neighboring one's did or so I heard. The police asked all of us, you see, and word gets around."

"I expect they've followed up on that," Pauline said. "And it doesn't help me with my quest to set Mrs. Common's mind at rest."

Gerry looked thoughtful. "Did you find a connection between the poverty gang and your dead man?"

"I did," Pauline said, her spirits rising. "Why?"

"Well," Gerry said, "one of the men in that group worked at that quarry, and not in the offices."

"Are you sure?"

He nodded. "Oh, aye. I've seen him around enough when the union is playing up at work."

"Do you know his name?" Pauline asked, trying not to show her excitement.

"I don't. He's not one of the union bosses, more of an enforcer, if you understand me."

"I do," Pauline said with a shudder.

"How does this help, Miss Riddell," Alf asked. "Harry Common wasn't a part of them, we all know that, so he couldn't have been involved in any bank raid."

"Harry's connection to those men was entirely different," Pauline said. "It's just now there's a connection between them and the bank robbery – or a possible connection, anyway."

"You think Harry saw the connection and they killed him?"

"I don't know, Alf," Pauline said. "It's just another link between the things that happened at the time."

"Like the Gospels being removed from view?" Gerry said suddenly. "Maybe, like the paper says, they may also have been stolen that night."

Pauline laughed in what she hoped was a convincing way. "You can't believe what you read in the papers, Gerry. Everybody knows that."

"But all we know about you, Miss Riddell, is what we read in the papers. Isn't that true?"

Pauline said seriously, "If you knew how much I disagreed with what the reporter wrote and how upset I was at the way everything was presented, you'd understand why I say don't believe the press."

"Some of what the journalist wrote must be true, Miss Riddell," Alf said, "or you wouldn't have the confidence of the police and the compliments of the judges in the cases."

"Some of it is true," Pauline agreed. "It's just that journalists write fiction around facts such that you can no longer tell which is real and which imaginary. If I didn't know who the articles were about, I wouldn't recognize me in them and that's the truth."

"What will you do now you know of this new connection?" one of the other men asked.

"I'll tell the police," Pauline said. "If they haven't already made the connection, they'll soon get to the bottom of it. It could be just a coincidence."

The men seemed to think this a very tame course of action and not what she should be doing. There were many comments about her chasing it down herself or leaving the 'plods' to find it for themselves.

"I told you I was misrepresented in the articles," Pauline replied, laughing. She bade them goodnight and left them to argue among themselves what she should or should not do. The discussion seemed likely to keep them going to quitting time.

Chapter Twenty-Six

CLOSING IN

AFTER THE DEBACLE over the religious group, the poverty group, and Sir Robert, Pauline was reluctant to volunteer more information but her duty, she knew, required it. Once home, she phoned Inspector Ramsay and explained what she'd learned.

He heard her out before saying, "You don't know who this man is, you don't know for certain he was among the poverty group, and you don't know he had anything to do with the dynamite going missing at that quarry. I can't take that very far, Miss Riddell."

"I do understand, Inspector," Pauline said. "I only pass it on in the hope somewhere in your investigation into that robbery, the name might have cropped up."

"You haven't got a name," Ramsay reminded her.

"But you did bring all the poverty group in for questioning, you must have their names and their occupations. They can't all be quarrymen. In fact, weren't they mainly metalworkers?"

"There are metalworkers at quarries, Miss Riddell, in

the maintenance side of the business. Unless we know where someone works, it won't help."

Pauline understood his reluctance. She'd been hesitant enough to tell him this, but now she had, she thought it a good lead and was frustrated at his lack of enthusiasm.

"The information the police took will have included where they worked, Inspector. That's vital knowledge."

"I'll see what we have and if there's any truth in it, have someone follow it up," Ramsay said. "The way things are right now I'll be lucky to have even that pass by my superiors."

"I'm going to see what other connections I can find to that group," Pauline said. "I didn't like them from the start. I should have trusted my instincts."

"If you find anything more, phone me," Ramsay said. "I'll need all the help I can get to push this through."

After hanging up, Pauline set to planning how she'd get this information she'd so lightly announced she'd find. If the men had been more friendly to the other protesters, they might have known. As it was, it was unlikely the protesters would know anything, and she knew no one else. It took a minute before she realized that Gerry knew the unknown quarryman, if only slightly, and Elsie of the Catholic women's group also said she knew one of the poverty group members. Could it be these two people were one person? If so, it was someone new because Gently was still in police custody. To now, he was the only one that could be shown to have committed a crime. Had she found another? It seemed another visit to the cathedral and the protesters was required.

Work dragged that next day, as it always seemed to do when she had something to investigate. Pauline's worry that one day she'd be fired because of her inability to concentrate on her job was growing, even while she couldn't stop thinking about her more exciting private interest.

Quitting time arrived and Pauline grabbed her coat and flew out of the door before Dr. Enderby found her work that meant staying back. The drive through rush hour was equally frustrating and it was an hour later she arrived at the cathedral. She was relieved to see all her usual contacts among the protesters were already in place.

It was the Northumbrian nationalists she came upon first. "Hello, Alf," Pauline said. "Is Gerry here tonight?" She couldn't see him among the group.

"He'll be here soon," Alf said. "His finishing time is later than ours and he has farther to come."

"I have to admire your determination on this," Pauline said. "Especially when you can't hope to get anything from it."

Alf laughed. "We didn't exist as a group when the visit of the Lindisfarne Gospels was announced. Now, we have a growing membership list and we're planning meetings and candidates for local council elections. We've done surprisingly well out of it."

"Then I wish you well," Pauline said. "I see someone over there." She pointed to the women chatting across the way. "I can talk to her until Gerry gets here."

She joined the group of women who, like the nationalists, were fewer in number tonight. The cold and damp were seeping into everyone's spirits, it seemed. She was greeted like a long-lost friend.

"I haven't come to protest," Pauline said, smiling. "I wanted a word with Elsie."

Elsie seemed put out at this and her expression became suspicious. "What about?"

"You knew of the man in Inspector Ramsay's photo,"

Pauline said. "I wondered if you knew anything more about him?"

"Such as?"

"Who his friends might be, for instance."

Elsie shook her head. "The only people I've seen him with are part of the gang who were here."

"Your aunt didn't mention anyone else who might be a friend or acquaintance?"

"My aunt isn't on speaking terms with the man," Elsie said. "She keeps herself and her bairns out of his way."

"She called him a wastrel," Pauline said. "But he has a job? He's in the same union that all the others of the poverty group seemed to be in. Why does she think he's a wastrel?"

"I can ask her," Elsie said, "or you could, if I introduced the two of you."

Pauline nodded. "That would be wonderful, Elsie, thank you."

"She may not want to meet you at her house," Elsie said, "in case you're recognized."

"What do you suggest?"

"I'll speak to her, and she can decide," Elsie said. "She doesn't have a car and she can't be away from her children too long. Her husband isn't good with bairns."

Pauline thought that sounded frightening but recognized it was likely only the true northern woman's reluctance to let her husband have any say in the management of her house and only a little of their children.

"Can you ask tomorrow and phone me here?" Pauline scribbled out her work phone number on a page from her notebook, which was sadly diminishing over the course of the past week. She handed it to Elsie.

"I will," Elsie said. "I'm not sure she'll help you though."

Seeing Gerry arriving, Pauline wished the women good night and hurried over to catch him before he joined Alf and his group.

"Gerry," she called, to stop him before he was close to the other men. "I have more questions."

"Of course, you do," he said good humoredly.

"You knew about the man who worked in a quarry," Pauline began.

"I knew he worked in a quarry," Gerry said. "That's about the extent of it."

"What does he do there?"

"He repairs or replaces metalwork that gets broken," Gerry replied. "So far as I know."

"Do you know if that's all there is? For example, would he order in more metal or ship out the metal you've replaced? Something like that?"

"If they're like us," Gerry said, "all the shipping in and out is done by others. We have contractors deliver fresh metal and take away scrap metal."

"Would it be worth anyone's while to steal the scrap?"

"Not the sheet steel," Gerry said, "but the copper and lead are worth money. Why, do you suspect him of thieving?"

Pauline laughed. "The police are holding someone they think is involved with the bank robbery that they haven't yet identified, and I wondered if your man may be him."

"You think he supplied the dynamite," Gerry said thoughtfully. "I don't know, but anything's possible, I reckon."

"Please don't tell people I believe this man you mention

is a criminal," Pauline said seriously. "It's just ideas I'm testing. It's not my considered opinion."

Gerry nodded. Pauline hoped he really would say nothing and bade him good night.

She should phone Ramsay when she got home, only she didn't want to. Tomorrow, after talking to Elsie's sister, she may have something worthwhile to tell. She hated this point in investigations when there were more questions than answers and even fewer leads to find answers.

However, her resolution was all in vain. Ramsay had phoned her and told Mrs. Bertram he'd call again, which he did.

"I phoned earlier," he said. "You weren't back from the cathedral. Were you able to discover anything?"

"Not really," Pauline said. "I'm to meet with a woman who lives on the same street as your suspect, and I hope to learn more from that. What about you?"

"You were right about him," Ramsay said. "His name is Joe Paisley, and he does work at the quarry where the explosives were found to be missing. I think we finally have a solid lead on our bank robbers."

"I hope the bank robbery will tie into the Gospels theft, which ties into Harry Common's death," Pauline said, "and that tomorrow night when we talk, we'll have all of it."

He laughed. "Your hope and enthusiasm are refreshing, Miss Riddell. Till tomorrow then."

Chapter Twenty-Seven

NEARLY DONE

THE PHONE on her desk rang and Pauline snatched it up. "Yes?" She couldn't risk Dr. Enderby picking it up in his office.

"It's Elsie, Pauline," the voice at the other end said. "Can you talk now?"

Dr. Enderby was writing a report. No one had dropped by in the past fifteen minutes, so Pauline said, "I can."

"Here's my sister," Elsie said. "She doesn't want to leave her neighborhood to talk. We're in the phone box at the end of her street."

"I hope you have plenty of change," Pauline said, but the line was already handed over.

"We have," the new voice said, "or at least Elsie has."

"I'll be quick," Pauline said. "Elsie said you called Joe Paisley a wastrel and that puzzles me for he has a job."

"He does, but he's more often hanging around the neighborhood than at it. He says he's on the sick."

"And is he sick?"

She laughed. "Not him. He's malingering, that's all."

"It must be difficult for his family if he has little money coming in. Sick pay isn't generous."

"He's a man of private means," the woman answered sarcastically. "Or at least, he has an income no one can quite see where it's from."

"He lives better than his wages would suggest?" Pauline asked.

"Nah! His family's as poor as church mice. He bets and drinks it away. He's never out of the bookies or the pub."

"How awful," Pauline said. "I can understand people making a bit on the side to feed their family but not to make bookies and landlords rich."

"Aye, well. That's how he is and nasty with it. No one here will let their kids play with his in case there's trouble," the woman said.

"You've no idea where his extra income comes from, have you?"

"The men say it comes from his work," she replied. "I wouldn't know."

"Is there anything else I should know?"

"Only that you'll be doing us all a favor if you put him inside," the woman said. "Even his own family would be better off in the end."

"I don't really know he's doing anything wrong," Pauline told her a little sadly. "There's just a lot of circum-stantial evidence that wouldn't stand up in court. And I can't link him at all to the death of Harry Common."

"Oh! I'd forgotten about that," the woman said. "There are people who heard him talking in the pub. Apparently, he said something like 'that man Common's death wasn't exactly accidental.' He was heard saying that 'yon man was a double-crossing'," she paused, before finishing lamely, "well, something not very polite, as you can imagine."

"Double cross," Pauline said. "Interesting. I wonder what that meant."

"No idea and he caught himself and hasn't said it again, so they say."

"Well, thank you for that," Pauline said. "You've given me lots to think about."

"Just get him, will you?"

"I'll do my best," Pauline replied. The telephone pips began, and the woman hung up the phone.

That evening, Ramsay phoned early. "I've good news, Miss Riddell," he said. "We've a connection now."

"Is it the scrap metal from the quarry, Inspector?"

"You've found it too," he said, laughing.

"Not exactly," Pauline said, and explained what she'd learned.

"I can fill in the rest," Ramsay said. "The scrap metal firm that picks up at those quarries is owned by a Mr. Croker of Newcastle. He's a villain we've never been able to catch."

"Joe Paisley knew him through his work, then," Pauline said.

"And probably sold stolen metal to him on the side, which is why Joe couldn't refuse when Croker encouraged him to steal the dynamite. Now we just have to sweat our Mr. Paisley and he'll talk, I'm sure of it."

"This is wonderful, Inspector," Pauline said. "It doesn't however explain how these people just walked into and out of the Lowther Bank to take the Gospels without breaking doors and windows."

"I think that will come out when he starts talking," Ramsay said. "Someone at the bank, and it can only be the manager, under-manager, or the three regular security guards, must be involved."

"Have you looked into the background of those people?"

"We have and they all seem to be regular people," Ramsay said. "But one of them clearly isn't as honest as the others."

"Is there any way I can help with them?"

"They're all sworn to secrecy about that night and the Gospels, Miss Riddell," Ramsay replied. "None of them should speak to you on this subject and none of them can have known Harry Common so I don't see how you can."

"These people know the Gospels are missing?" Pauline asked.

"The one in on the theft does," Ramsay said. "The others have been told not to spread or add to the malicious rumors they're hearing in the press."

"That would surely convince them there's something behind all this."

"They're suspicious, I'm sure," Ramsay said. "However, I think for the most part they have bought into the story that there was no theft, and we have to squash the rumor that there was."

"I can't help feeling it would have been better to have told the truth," Pauline said. "It really constrains the investigation pretending it's about other things."

"The powers that be panicked and plucked that denial out of the air," Ramsay said, "and now we're stuck with it. I think the idea was the thieves would ask for money right away, the authorities would pay, and this would all be over in a day."

"I'm going to ask the two managers if they recognize Harry or the man who killed him," Pauline said. "That may lead me to something more."

"They aren't implicated in anything to do with Harry's death," Ramsay protested. "It wasn't even near their bank."

"I shall say I've reason to believe Harry Common was linked to one of their customers," Pauline said.

"He was actually," Ramsay admitted. "Sir Robert Lauriston has an account there but so do many others."

"Anyone we're interested in?"

"Yes, Sir Arthur Warkworth and one of his metals businesses has an account there."

"I wish you'd told me this before," Pauline said. "It opens the field to many possible alternatives."

"The Task Force has followed up on both these men and the link to the bank," Ramsay said. "They are convinced both men are innocent, even more so now we made a hash of that false lead."

"Warkworth's metals business couldn't link him to Harry Common, could it?" Pauline asked.

"Hardly, Miss Riddell," Ramsay said. "The business deals in the sale and recycling of scrap metals. It doesn't sell to individual tradesmen. Anyway, as I said, it was investigated and dismissed. You should dismiss it too."

"Hmm," Pauline said derisively. "I wouldn't trust that Task Force with anything important."

"Then I've led you into being prejudiced against them," Ramsay said. "And I'm sorry. They are very capable officers with years of experience. They may be rubbing me and most of the local men up the wrong way, but you shouldn't judge by that."

"If you say so, Inspector. I'm still going to the bank to meet those managers, though. What can you tell me about them?"

"They're both local men, grew up in the Durham area

and have no criminal records, not even parking tickets. They are the very epitome of bank managers."

"They couldn't have met Harry or his killer at school or growing up?"

"Harry went to school and lived all his life out in Weardale," Ramsay said. "They grew up in and around the city of Durham. The under-manager is very much a local success story. From a poor family, did well at school, went to college, before finding employment in the bank and working his way up."

"The manager?"

"More usual route to the top," Ramsay said. "Leafy suburbs, grammar school, university, and then the bank."

"I have my question for the two managers," Pauline said. "I'll let you know if I learn anything new." She hung up the phone and planned her next steps.

Chapter Twenty-Eight

A BREAKTHROUGH BECKONS

THE FOLLOWING MORNING, when Dr. Enderby was out of his office, Pauline called Lowther's Bank asking to speak to the manager. After she'd explained who she was and after some hesitation on his part, he agreed to an interview at lunchtime.

Pauline was there in good time, hoping she could meet both managers before her lunch hour was over. She was ushered into his office, a seat offered, the door closed.

Pauline began. "As I mentioned on the phone, Mr. Mitchell, I'm looking into the recent death of Harry Common, not far away from here. Just up the street, to be exact."

"I read about it, of course," he replied, "but I don't know how I can help."

"Did you know him?"

"No. Not at all," he said.

"I thought he might have come to this bank because he often worked for Sir Robert Lauriston who banks here.

Maybe your tellers might recognize his photo?" She showed him the photo provided by Mrs. Common.

"We can certainly ask," he said. "However, I think it unlikely Sir Robert would allow someone like Mr. Common to do his banking. His secretary is often here but never a hired hand."

"It is a faint hope," Pauline agreed. "It's just Harry's mother would like some comfort there was nothing amiss and her son's death really was an accident."

"We're a small bank and don't have many tellers," he said. "I could ask those who are free right now to step in here and look at the photo, if you wish."

"Please," Pauline said. "That would be helpful. My investigations so far haven't turned up anything untoward but I do want to be thorough. Poor woman, she's quite distraught."

He rose and said, while walking to the door, "I can imagine. If anything happened to either of my children, I'd be grief stricken." He stepped outside and returned a moment later.

"Here's our Mrs. Joyce," he said, introducing a motherly woman to Pauline.

Mrs. Joyce's keen eyes flicked over the photo, and she shook her head. "No. I've never seen him in here."

Pauline thanked her.

"It's lunchtime right now, Miss Riddell," Mitchell said as Mrs. Joyce left, "and we're busy. I've asked the others to come in but only if they don't have customers to serve. You understand, I hope."

Pauline nodded. "I'm on my lunch hour too. Is the under-manager here?"

"He's gone for lunch," Mitchell said. "He and I share

responsibilities over the lunch period so we each get fed. Maybe if you returned after we close?"

"Thank you," Pauline said, relieved. "Will four-thirty be too late?"

"It is late," Mitchell said, "but I'm sure some of the staff will be happy to wait. At least one has children to pick up at school, you see."

"Then I'll return as early as I can," Pauline said, preparing to go.

DR. ENDERBY WAS NOT enthusiastic when Pauline asked to leave early.

"This is still your place of work, Pauline," he said, as he gave her permission to go. "Are you sure you still want to work here?"

"I do, Dr. Enderby," Pauline said. "I don't often ask for time off. I'll make it up tomorrow night or, if there's something you need urgently, I'll come back later."

"There's nothing right now," he said. "I just see a falling off in your interest and performance that I want you to know I'm aware of."

He really knows how to make me feel guilty, Pauline thought somewhat resentfully.

"I'll make this my last investigation," Pauline said. "I promise." And she really meant it, at that moment.

At three, she shot out of the factory and raced through the growing traffic to the bank, where she found the staff carrying out their closing routines.

Mitchell let her into the bank and introduced her to his assistant, the under-manager.

"Thank you for talking with me," Pauline said, shaking his hand. "I realize this isn't everyone's cup of tea."

The man laughed nervously. "We've had the police here so often these past days, we're almost at the point of missing it when it stops."

Pauline smiled. "My question is much easier to answer," she said, handing him the photo. "Did you ever see this man in the bank?"

The under-manager studied the photo before handing it back. "No, I'm sure he isn't a customer of ours."

"What about this man," Pauline said on an impulse. She removed the photo of Joe Paisley from the envelope and handed it over.

"No, not him either," the man said. His expression was secretive, and he looked away to the manager. "I don't think we have any customers who look like either of these men."

"I didn't see the second photo, Miss Riddell," the manager said, holding out his hand and taking it.

He considered the photo carefully. "You're right, Frank. Not one of ours."

Pauline took the photo back and handed them all the photos she had. "Do you recognize any of these faces?" She looked closely at the manager, while keeping the under-manager's face in the corner of her eye. She was right. The man recognized one or more members of the poverty action group.

"I'm sorry, Miss Riddell," the manager said, after he'd looked at all the photos, "none of these men look familiar."

The under-manager returned his copies to her and agreed, "Again, none of these men are our customers."

The tellers all confirmed what the managers had said. The men weren't customers, and they hadn't been in the bank, to their knowledge.

"Then I'm sorry to have wasted your time," Pauline said.

Mitchell laughed. "It's like Frank said, we're so used to it now, we're going to miss all the excitement when it's gone."

"By the way," Pauline said, as she turned to leave, "there's really no truth in the rumor the Gospels were stolen from here, is there?"

Both managers looked shocked. "Absolutely none, Miss Riddell. You shouldn't believe everything you read in the papers, you know."

Pauline smiled. "The articles speak of rumors. I expect it is just the usual gossip."

Mitchell held open the door for her as she left the bank. "Yes, gossip is truly awful, and those articles are causing us a lot of bother. I can't go anywhere now without being questioned about it. For a bank and a banker, it's most distressing."

Pauline returned to her car and joined the rush hour traffic heading north, arriving home so early Mrs. Bertram was shocked to see her.

"Are you all right, dear? You're not ill, are you?"

"I'm fine," Pauline said. "I just got away early today, that's all."

"Well, you do need a rest," Mrs. Bertram said. "You work all day and then investigate all evening and weekends. It's not wise."

"I agree," Pauline said, hanging up her coat and setting off up the stairs to her room. "I'm making this my last case. It's messy and there's no clear-cut answer that I can see. These things are best left to the police."

"I'm glad to hear you say that," Mrs. Bertram said. "Now you nap while I get dinner ready."

Pauline lay on her bed but didn't nap. She calculated Inspector Ramsay wouldn't be home early tonight, which meant she'd have to wait hours to phone or be phoned. She sat up, grabbed her much slimmed down notepad and made notes of today's interviews. It created a new question only the police could easily answer.

It was long after nine before Ramsay called and Pauline's nerves were taut by then. Waiting to make progress was the most painful part of investigating.

"Joe Paisley was persuaded to steal the dynamite for Croker," Ramsay said. "Mr. Croker denies it and was still denying it when I left. The London men are working on him in shifts. We should have something by morning. What about you, Miss Riddell?"

"I don't like the sound of those London men working on Mr. Croker," Pauline answered.

"He's an unpleasant man who isn't above working on others, Miss Riddell," Ramsay said. "It's best we focus on what's important."

"I have a question, Inspector," Pauline said, recognizing no good would come from continuing her complaint about methods. "Where did the under-manager grow up?"

"I told you, in the Durham area."

"I mean specifically where," Pauline said. "I think he knew some of the poverty group. He was evasive when I showed him their photos. They may have leaned on him to let them into the bank that night."

"I knew having someone look deeper into those protesters would pay dividends," Ramsay said. "I'll have it checked out overnight. The night shift has nothing to do in Durham. It's sleepy enough by day. The nights are comatose."

"Your big city prejudice is showing, Inspector. Those Londoners would say the same about Newcastle."

He laughed. "Maybe, but unlike me, they'd be wrong."

"I wish I could be sure which of the men the under-manager recognized," Pauline continued. "Only, they were all on the one photo and I didn't want to alert him I'd seen the recognition in his eyes."

"They are the four you saw in the Wheatsheaf though," Ramsay said.

"Yes, and their leader Temperley was in the photo, too. I'd bet it was him – if I were a betting woman."

"That lanky streak of misery is the easiest to recognize, I agree," Ramsay said.

"The question I still have, Inspector, is how the Gospels thieves knew of the bank robbery or is it a single planner? A coordinated robbery or did they find out about the bank robbery?"

"I think a single plan," Ramsay said. "It makes the most sense."

"Paisley talked when he had too much to drink," Pauline replied. "I think it could have been your Newcastle thieves acting alone but one of the so-called anti-poverty gang heard Paisley talking and they saw their opportunity."

"It's possible," Ramsay said. "As soon as I hear how the day went, I'll phone you. I think this time we may have it wrapped up, Miss Riddell."

It was mid-morning before Ramsay phoned, and Pauline was busy on a report for Dr. Enderby. "I can't talk now, Inspector," Pauline said, seeing her boss's eyes coldly watching her. "I'll phone you at lunchtime."

At lunch, Pauline walked out of the factory to the nearby phone box and called. Her conscience pricked her. She'd promised to focus on her work. Too many more of these interruptions and Dr. Enderby would rightfully come to see her as being uninterested in her job.

Fortunately, Ramsay was at his desk. "I have even better news now, Miss Riddell," he said. "Not only has Croker pointed a finger at our Mr. Graystoke, but you were right. Temperley and the under-manager grew up on the same street. We're interviewing them both even as we speak."

"You say 'we're' interviewing them, Inspector, but you're talking to me," Pauline said uncomfortably.

"Our senior officers have taken over the running of my bank robbery investigation, now that it looks like it has links to the other theft and there's the chance of medals to be handed out."

"I don't like it," Pauline said flatly.

"This will all be wrapped up by the end of the day, the Gospels will be found, and you and I can return to our own lives. Anything that helps that along, must be good in my estimation."

"You will ensure they stay within the law, won't you?" Pauline asked.

"Unlike some, I believe in the law," Ramsay said. "I'll see it is observed wherever I am."

"Then I look forward to hearing it's over," Pauline said. "The Gospels are returned, the bank robbers are behind bars, and whoever put them up to it has also been arrested."

"Mr. Graystoke will sell his buyer to save his skin, never you fear," Ramsay said. "Until tonight then."

Pauline returned to the factory and her office with a feeling of relief. Now she might see the real Gospels and be able to compare. And now she could hang up her tin star, as they said in the cowboy movies.

Chapter Twenty-Nine

WRONG AGAIN

HER EVENING PHONE call with Ramsay, however, threw her back into turmoil. Mr. Graystoke had, after finally understanding the wisdom of helping the police with their inquiries, identified Sir Arthur Warkworth as the man who managed the attempted theft of the Gospels. Warkworth, when questioned with his expensive lawyer present, forcefully denied everything.

Worse, Graystoke said they did use Harry Common and Temperley to steal the Gospels, but they were too late, someone had already exchanged the cases and they carried away a case that, when opened later, was empty except for a sheet of lead used as a weight.

The under-manager swore Temperley had threatened his wife and family to force him into taking part, but he let only Harry Common into the bank vault that night and he had no idea how the switch had been made.

Once again, the Task Force were able to fast-track search warrants and began the long process of searching

Graystoke's Gallery, Temperley's house, Mrs. Common's cottage, and Sir Arthur's home.

Even as the search was beginning, Ramsay had returned to his small band of detectives and set them on investigating an idea he'd been mulling over for days, which didn't make him popular with the men. They too had been expecting to go home to their families on time.

Pauline was also wracking her brains, going through her notes and memories to find a solution. Her thoughts came down to if the successful thieves haven't yet been caught and she had misgivings about the results of the searches, then she needed to know who ordered the second attaché case. According to Graystoke, the poverty group only ordered one. There was someone not yet identified.

By midnight, it was clear to the Task Force and the Chief Commissioner that none of the places searched was where the Gospels were hidden. The Chief Constable convened a meeting of senior officers and sent the rest of the team home.

With the Warkworth lead fizzled out and Sir Arthur angrily threatening retaliation, the police were looking at repercussions from someone with standing, not only locally but even down in London. The Task Force leader had already handed the investigation back to Ramsay.

"Well, Ramsay," the Chief Constable said. "How was it we searched Sir Arthur's home on what amounts to no more than the word of a known criminal?"

Ramsay, who'd been expecting this to be on him and had practiced an answer, replied firmly, "Julian Graystoke was not a known criminal, sir. And, if you recall, I'd been asked to oversee the team wrapping up the evidence by the time the warrant was requested. It wasn't my intention to ask for a warrant until we had gathered more evidence." He maintained a steady gaze on the Commissioner and the Task Force leader sitting next to him.

"He's an admitted known criminal now and you assured us he was known to the Newcastle police," the leader said.

"Nevertheless," Ramsay said, "to continue answering your question, Commissioner, we did have some reason to request a warrant, even if I wasn't consulted. There was every possibility that, hearing of the arrests of Paisley and Temperley, the holder of the Gospels might have moved them. I feel we'll be safe from Sir Arthur's recriminations, in the end."

"I hope you're right, Ramsay," the Commissioner said, leaving Ramsay in no doubt he'd been selected as the scapegoat if things did go badly. "It's been a long day. Have we anything new to start on tomorrow?"

"We'll continue interviewing Graystoke and Temperley," the leader said. "They will have had a whole night to consider their options, so we'll get more tomorrow. I am confident of that."

"Anyone else?"

"I hesitate to put anything forward in the current climate," Ramsay said. "But I do have something to follow up."

"Never mind that bolshie nonsense," the Commissioner said, testily. "Out with it."

"A tramp steamer left Sunderland at 6:30 on the morning tide following the robbery. My men have traced it to Brest, and we've asked Interpol to have the captain speak to us in the morning."

"You think the Gospels went straight from the bank to this ship and are now out of the country?"

"I don't think anything at this stage, sir," Ramsay said. "Only that it's a possibility we need to look into."

The Commissioner turned angrily to the Task Force leader. "Why wasn't this picked up at the time?"

The leader, his face bland though his voice oozed fury, said, "I don't know, Commissioner. After all, I and my team didn't arrive here until after midday that day. Why wasn't it investigated *at the time*?"

The Commissioner was momentarily taken aback but recovered quickly. "It should have been, and it should have been one of the Task Force's first avenues of investigation when they discovered it hadn't been."

Ramsay, feeling he'd done enough for now to put the two allies against him at odds with each other, said, "Even if we speak to the captain, he won't be mad enough to admit having taken a passenger on board at this stage. We've plans to interview the coastguard and military in case they noticed the ship behaving oddly."

"In what way, odd?"

"It may have halted to let a passenger get off on a boat, either on the English side of the sea or the Dutch side, for example."

"You think it may be back in this country but somewhere farther south?" the Commissioner asked.

"It's possible," Ramsay said, "though my guess is it's on the continent and we won't see it again in our lifetimes."

"Get your men on it first thing, Ramsay," the Commissioner said, "and give him some more men." This last was addressed to the Task Force leader.

The meeting broke up. As he left the building the Task Force leader grabbed Ramsay by the arm and said, "You think that stunt was funny?"

Ramsay removed his arm from the man's grip and replied. "I was keeping you all informed on my progress. If you'd given me the opportunity before we went into the meeting, you wouldn't have been surprised."

"You may be a somebody up here, my friend, but in our neck of the woods we eat folks like you for breakfast. Undermining your superiors will come back to haunt you, you see if it doesn't."

The man strode angrily back to his posse of subordinates who eyed Ramsay with the same loathing they saw in their leader's face. Ramsay walked down the street to a nearby hotel. There wasn't time to waste commuting home.

Chapter Thirty

THE CASE WRAPS UP

THROUGHOUT THE MORNING, the Task Force worked on the known criminals – Graystoke, Temperley, Gently and Paisley – while Ramsay and his men interviewed the ship's captain, who claimed to know nothing. They followed up the interview by questioning the military and coastguard organizations. They had no records to suggest the ship had done anything out of the ordinary on its voyage from Sunderland to Rotterdam. It was another dead end.

Wishing he'd never mentioned this possibility, Ramsay dragged himself unwillingly to the meeting called by the Chief Commissioner to begin at noon.

The commissioner, however, had either made up his mind or it had been made up for him. After running through the information given to him by his subordinates, he summed it up. "We'll continue with the charges against the two sets of bank robbers and your dodgy art dealer, Ramsay," he said.

Ramsay noted that Graystoke was definitely 'his' again and said nothing.

The commissioner continued, "What our report to the government will say is this: an international dealer, and the search for him will continue at a lower level of intensity, used the greed of the poverty group to steal the Lindisfarne Gospels. They thought he was buying the book from them. However, he had an accomplice among the gang, likely Harry Common, who switched the Gospel case for an identical case he'd made. The identical case was weighted so the thieves didn't notice the switch right away."

He paused glaring around the table daring anyone to object before continuing, "The accomplice took the real case and Gospels straight to the international dealer and was paid. The dealer left on the ship that sailed before the theft was even discovered. The dealer was dropped off on the Dutch coast before the ship docked in Rotterdam. The Gospels are in the hands of an unidentified collector, almost certainly on the continent and they will likely never be seen again. Interpol will be asked to follow up. When the thieves discovered they'd been hoodwinked, they killed Harry Common. Case closed."

Ramsay felt an overwhelming sense of relief. Though it traduced poor Harry Common without any evidence, this outcome, almost certainly approved at the highest levels, meant he could go home and get on with proper policing. He didn't care what rich people did for trinkets that meant nothing to everyday people. People were what mattered, not relics.

"However," the Commissioner continued in a voice laden with menace, "the government will likely release their own statement and it may not entirely align with what we're reporting. I would remind you all to remember we are servants of the government, and we keep our opinions on this matter to ourselves. Is that clear?"

There was a general muttering of agreement that seemed to satisfy the Commissioner and he called an end to the meeting.

Back at his desk, the phone was ringing. DS Morrison had found Poppy, who was living in squalid student digs not far from the University. Did Ramsay want her brought in for questioning?

"No," Ramsay said. "Give me the address and Miss Riddell can have a crack at making her see sense."

Pauline however, when she was told where to find Poppy, was less than enthusiastic.

"I think it should be you, Inspector," she said. "She might listen to you when she won't listen to me."

"I say we compromise," Ramsay said. "We go together. Maybe having all three of us back together will stir happy memories."

Pauline reluctantly agreed. She couldn't help remembering Poppy's expression at their last meeting.

DS Morrison's description of the digs was, if anything, too kind. An old house in a blackened, unloved row of houses was where Ramsay and Pauline met after work. The house's door opened right onto the street, its paint almost gone, and the curtains at the windows were simply rags. The whole street appeared to be given over to students, many of whom watched them with suspicious expressions as they knocked on the door.

A young man opened the door. He was at least presentable, Pauline thought. His trousers had been pressed, his shirt was clean, and his tie looked like an old school tie rather than one from the cheaper end of the flea market.

"Is Poppy in?" Pauline asked.

"She's not here," he said. "She's gone."

"Gone?" Pauline said. "Will she be back later?"

"No, she's gone," the man said. "She heard someone was looking for her and she took off."

"When was this?"

"I don't know," he replied. "She left a note for me. I found it when I came back from the afternoon lectures."

"Did she say where she's gone?" Pauline asked. "I really need to speak to her."

He smiled. "You're Pauline Riddell." His tone was triumphant.

"I am and I'm a friend of Poppy's."

He laughed. "In your mind maybe. Poppy sees it differently."

"That's why I need to see her," Pauline said. "To straighten out the rift between us. Did she say where she was going?"

He shook his head. "No and I wouldn't tell you if she had." He closed the door with a firm thump that shook its rotted frame.

"I'll have some surveillance on this place tonight," Ramsay said as they returned to their cars. "I don't believe she's gone.

"I hope you're right, Inspector," Pauline said, "but I think we have no hope of stopping her. You won't tell your bosses yet, will you?"

"No," he said. "Not yet."

Chapter Thirty-One

TO THE FUTURE

WITH THE GOSPELS investigation officially over, and both escaping from it unharmed, Pauline and Ramsay met for drinks in their usual pub the next evening.

"I'm back at my own station, Miss Riddell, and I hope never to see or hear of the Lindisfarne Gospels again in my life."

"You must be happy to finally have Mr. Croker and Mr. Graystoke locked up though, Inspector," Pauline said.

"They aren't behind bars yet," Ramsay said. "They're out on bail and we're still building our case, but yes, I very much hope they will be soon."

"And has this success offset your bosses' feelings over our leading them astray with Warkworth and Lauriston?"

"It has. All that's forgotten now they've shuffled off the ugly part. The results we actually achieved are in some measure down to me, and my boss has recommended me for promotion," Ramsay said. "I wish I could share some of the goodwill with you, Miss Riddell, but unless you join the force, I'm afraid you'll have to live with my simple thank you."

Pauline laughed. "That's good enough for me," she said. "You invited me to help, and it's been an amazing experience, one I would never have had otherwise. I think we're in each other's debt, Inspector."

"Did you ever get to speak to Poppy?" Ramsay asked.

Pauline shook her head. "I tried again but no, did you?" When he said he hadn't, Pauline continued, "I think she has now gone to London, and I'll leave it. If she wants to get in touch, she knows where to find me."

"I saw another article by our 'northern correspondent' yesterday in the Telegraph. You could phone them and ask for her address."

Pauline shook her head. "The rift is too great, Inspector. She really went after me in that article, didn't you think?"

Ramsay nodded, sadly. "Here's to the future, then, Miss Riddell." They clinked glasses and drank to themselves.

Chapter Thirty-Two

APOLOGY

ONCE AGAIN, Pauline stood outside the imposing doors of Sir Robert's house waiting for the butler to let her in. She only hoped the butler had no suspicion of her treatment of his master. She was fairly confident the master of the house would forgive her; she was sure his servants wouldn't. She'd gained a strong impression of how the staff felt about him on her previous visit.

The door opened and the butler invited her in with due ceremony. She couldn't say if that meant he knew or didn't. He was a very correct butler, even if he was reduced to also doing a footman's job. Pauline wondered if that had cost him any anguish or if he was philosophical about the reduced standards that the postwar economy had forced on everyone.

He led her again into the conservatory where Sir Robert was reading his newspaper.

"Miss Riddell," he said, rising and extending his hand. "You're in good time."

"I'm early because I want to put this out of the way as soon as I can. My visit, you see, is one that causes me some discomfort, Sir Robert," Pauline said, shaking his hand but ignoring his offer of a seat. He may not want her to stay when he heard what she had to say.

"You're here to arrest me?" he asked, grinning.

She shook her head. "Nothing so open and honest, I'm afraid. The search of your house and buildings was due to information I provided the police. It can't have been pleasant for you or your staff, and I was wrong. I've come to offer my apologies."

He smiled. "Apology accepted, Miss Riddell. Now please, sit down and tell me everything. I'll have some tea brought in or would you prefer coffee? I know so many do in the morning."

"Tea would be nice, thank you," Pauline said, settling herself in the well-cushioned colonial chair.

He rang a bell, and in a few moments, the maid arrived. He ordered and waited for the woman to leave before saying, "Now, explain your reasons for turning me in like that."

Pauline gave him her reasoning based on what she'd seen and heard. He didn't seem in the least upset and they chatted amicably until the tea arrived. Pauline found she desperately wanted to tell him about the midnight search of his ruined castle but as Ramsay was involved, and he would be in more danger of retaliation than she was, she let it stay unconfessed.

"Do you often get these things wrong, Miss Riddell?"

"I haven't investigated many things, Sir Robert, but of the three I have, I can say I've made lots of false deductions. Inspector Ramsay says the police do too so I shouldn't be downhearted about my mistakes but I am."

"He has experience," Sir Robert said. "You should listen to his advice. Tell me, have the Gospels been stolen?"

"The police have been investigating a robbery at a great house where there were many art treasures stolen," Pauline said. "That's all I can say."

"I wondered," Sir Robert replied. "There's a journalist who swears they have, and you were investigating the theft."

"I'm trying to set Mrs. Common's mind at ease over Harry's death, nothing more," Pauline said. "The bank robbery and the rumors about the Gospels all seemed to be part of one giant conspiracy at times. My blundering investigations have touched on all of them to my own and others' consternation."

"And were they linked?"

"I'm afraid so," Pauline said. "Whether he knew it or not, Harry was making the fake case the Gospels *were to be* spirited away in. Somehow, he and the people who commissioned the case fell out and he was killed." She stressed *were to be* in the hope it would sound as if she believed it.

"You don't think Harry knew what the case was for?"

"I've told Mrs. Common I don't," Pauline said. "However, he was making a second, identical case for someone else and I think that means he knew." She stared hard into Sir Robert's eyes, hoping to see a flicker of what? Guilt?

"I'm sure Harry was working for the good of everyone in the north, Miss Riddell," Sir Robert said. "He probably realized what the case was going to be used for and made the second for himself."

"Perhaps but that means the Gospels *were* stolen and someone has them," Pauline said. "Or Harry was in on the theft, made the switch after and has hidden them away somewhere we can't find. Do you know any place Harry might put them for safety?"

He shook his head. "I don't. But if they *were* stolen, I know Harry would make sure they were safe, and they'll come to light one day. Like the story about Drake's Drum, they'll appear whenever the country is in danger."

"I would have thought someone such as yourself would understand how delicate artifacts are and how carefully they need to be kept. I doubt Harry would have such a hiding place."

"I would trust Harry to put them in a safe place, Miss Riddell, if he did indeed steal them. He knew how important the preservation of artifacts is. We talked about it often enough. However, to be a little contrarian in this matter, the Gospels book survived over a thousand years without any modern preservation processes whatever. Would a few more years matter?"

"You would know better than I about that, Sir Robert," Pauline said, amused at this verbal jousting. "And you can't think of anywhere they may be?"

"I'm sorry," he said. "As I said once before, Harry and I weren't partners. I wasn't privy to all his secrets so I don't know where Harry might have hidden the book. If it is in fact missing."

"If the real Gospels are hidden, think of all the people who will miss seeing them," Pauline said. "Generations who will only see a replica."

"I've no problem with that, Miss Riddell. They won't know the difference and to be honest, they won't care even if they did."

"But is it ethical letting millions of people file past the Gospels in the British Museum thinking they are seeing the real thing?"

"They probably file past many copies in the British Museum and many other great repositories around the

world every day because the wear and tear on the originals is too much," he replied, smiling. "It's sad but the deception is in everyone's best interest, especially for the people of the future who will have the originals to study in ways we today can only dream of, which they wouldn't if the originals are destroyed by age and decay. For example, I read the other day that Tutankhamun's tomb is already deteriorating because of the number of visitors. Likewise, the relics from the tomb."

"You think it's best the Gospels be kept hidden if they were stolen?"

"Not forever," he said. "Only until the time is right for them to be displayed where they belong. And that can only come after they are found, *if they were stolen*, or after the government decides to trust us here in the north with what is actually our own inheritance."

Pauline sipped her tea as she thought on her next step. When she'd finished, she said, "Sir Robert, I'm sorry to ask, but have you or have you not got the Lindisfarne Gospels?"

He laughed. "You have my permission to search the house and grounds from now until Doomsday, Miss Riddell. Bring the police too."

"You didn't answer my question," Pauline said.

"You have the only answer I intend to give," he replied. "Now can I interest you in another look at my collection? So few people ask to see them, and I do feel you owe me the opportunity to bore you for an hour on the subject of my antiquities, as a penance."

Pauline smiled. "I'd like that," she said, "and I'm sure you won't bore me. In fact, I'm tempted to donate my flint arrowhead to your collection before my mother throws it out in a future spring cleaning."

"I shall display it proudly in the center of my Neolithic

relics," he said. "With a notice saying *Donated by the Famous Miss Riddell.*"

Chapter Thirty-Three

THE STORY ENDS

"IT'S Miss Riddell's story to tell," Ramsay said, shaking his head. "I just help her along."

They were all gathered in Theresa Thompson's best sitting room. It was quite a squeeze for the church ladies and the Northumbrian nationalists were both in attendance. It was fortunate the two groups had become close through their weeks of protesting.

"That's nonsense," Pauline said, briskly. "Without Inspector Ramsay, there'd be no story to tell."

"Nevertheless," Ramsay said, "we're all ears. You'll tell it much better than I would."

"Very well. First, I should say at the outset I had no idea who had intended to steal the Gospels. None of the participants in the drama had any sensible motive or opportunity to steal them. Inspector Ramsay only asked me to meet with Harry Common's mother to see if I could learn something the police hadn't."

"But the police were asking about missing art works, weren't they, Inspector?" Alf asked.

"We were," Ramsay said, "but the connection to Harry Common's death wasn't there."

"Never mind all that," Theresa said, addressing Pauline. "Why did you decide it wasn't us who tried to steal the Gospels, or the treasure, whatever the treasure was? Are you one of these folks who think women can't do things?"

Pauline laughed. "It would be strange if I were. No, I kept you and your church ladies on my list of possible villains for a long time, particularly when Inspector Ramsay told me of your wartime service. Although, like the police, I didn't see the connection right away. When I did, I thought I finally had the answer there."

"Oh good," Theresa said happily. "We could have done, you know. It's nice to feel one isn't entirely overlooked when one has grown older. I sometimes feel I've disappeared. As though I wasn't there. Like the 'man on the stair' in the old rhyme."

Pauline smiled. "I'm sure no one would ever think you weren't there, Theresa. You're such a nuisance. I expect you'll be murdered one day."

"If I am, I'll have it in my will that *you* have to investigate," Theresa said. "We nuisances must stick together."

"Miss Riddell isn't a nuisance, Mrs. Thompson," Ramsay protested. "At least, not to those in the know."

"Then I won't repeat what your Scotland Yard man said when he was interrogating me," Theresa said sharply.

"But he isn't in the know," Ramsay said. "He's from London."

"Can we get back to my story?" Pauline said. Though she always demurred when people asked her to explain, she suddenly found she was irritated that the attention had drifted away.

"Of course, Pauline," Theresa said contritely. "Do carry on."

Now she was bidden to continue, Pauline found she didn't want to, but she began, "Following up on your group, I discovered a lot of interesting facts. You told me the bank manager was a friend. What you didn't say was he was a member of the same congregation or that your local priest was an Irishman with strong political as well as religious views."

Theresa nodded. "Father O' Reilly is very interested in the history of the early Irish missionaries to the heathen Anglo-Saxons, and the Celtic influences in both Northumbria and the Lindisfarne Gospels. All that's true, but he would never suggest stealing them. He'd be shocked to learn you thought he would. He's a very upright man."

"It would be a bit obvious, Mrs. Thompson," Ramsay said. "I think even the Scotland Yard man may have spotted the connection if your priest had suggested it."

"Leaving aside the inter-force bickering," Pauline said severely, "I did decide you and your group were very credible suspects, which is why you were brought in for questioning. I'm sorry about that."

"Don't be, dear," Theresa said. "You can't imagine how many times I've wished to use the anti-interrogation training we received back at the SOE. I was fortunately never caught and never had to use it then." She paused, and added sadly, "I daresay, I'd have cracked. Most of us did." She paused again. Then, suddenly brightening, said, "But when I was hauled in by the police, a dawn raid too, it was a dream come true."

"Then I'm pleased my poor deductions gave you some pleasure and not pain," Pauline said, laughing.

"Fortunately for me, the police aren't allowed to use any unpleasant techniques. Also, we were innocent."

"When that was shown to be true," Pauline said, "I remembered an earlier thought I'd had around the death of Harry Common. It had seemed so unlikely to be a coincidence at the time and yet there was nothing to link him with the disappearance of the Gospels."

"What changed your mind?" Theresa asked.

"Just a growing realization there must be a connection," Pauline said. "It was the only way any of this made sense."

"And he was?"

Pauline nodded. "Yes, his mother and Sir Robert had already told me he'd worked at Lauriston's mine when it was nationalized. And he was laid off when the mine closed. That wasn't news. What I learned was he continued working for Sir Robert and shared an interest in antiquities and devolved rule for the north of England."

"He was probably one of them agitating for nationalization," Alf said, "so my sympathy isn't roused a great deal."

"You do Harry wrong, Alf. He tried to persuade the miners to campaign against it," Pauline said. "When the mine closed, Sir Robert who thought highly of Harry, continued to give him work on his estate and other projects."

"Was it just Harry Common who was angry?" Theresa asked. "I imagine Sir Robert was too."

Pauline nodded. "You're right. Sir Robert was as angry about what happened to his mine and his workers as the workers were themselves. He found odd jobs for many of them to do on his estate, his cars, and his farm machinery."

"So, Harry wasn't so special then?" Alf asked.

"Not particularly in that regard but it was a link to a

collector of antiquities and to one who shared the same political leanings."

"Ugh, politics," Ramsay said.

Pauline smiled. "Quite so, Inspector, politics. When I talked to Sir Robert, he made no secret that he was also a campaigner for more autonomy for the north."

Theresa said, "When we were cleared, you switched to Harry Common and the poverty activists?"

Pauline nodded. "That seemed to be a telling link."

"Why not his more obvious link to Sir Robert?" Ramsay asked.

Pauline flushed pink. "Honestly, I see now it was because I liked Sir Robert and disliked the union men. So, I jumped on the union link not the rich collector link. It was very wrong of me."

"But there was plenty to suggest you were right in singling out that lot," Ramsay said. "Poverty activists, indeed; some people have no shame at all. Only out for themselves and quite capable of theft when it suits them."

"Exactly," Pauline said, nodding. "My wrong turning here wasn't entirely misplaced. Bye the bye, Inspector, I hope you've had the bank make the changes to ensure pressure can't be brought to bear on any other of their staff members?"

"They've made the changes we suggested," Ramsay said.

Pauline took up the story again. "Once again, however, I hadn't quite got it right and the police had to let them go. That was embarrassing for me and," Pauline paused, smiling at Ramsay, then adding, "even worse for Inspector Ramsay. Later, as you know, the ringleaders were arrested but others remain free. If they suspect my hand in their arrest, my own freedom will be circumscribed until it's all blown over."

"Make sure you're never alone or in the wrong part of town," Ramsay said. "We'll keep an eye on your lodgings and be on hand as you enter and leave the factory. Once the trial is over, you'll come out of it just fine."

"I wish I shared your confidence, Inspector," Pauline said. "Anyway, with the end of that trail, I was left without an idea in my head. The only thing that kept me going was the police hadn't solved the puzzle either."

Ramsay nodded. "The trouble with policing is we encounter a higher proportion of criminals than the average citizen and that colors our view of people and events. What a regular person may see as innocent mistakes or accidents, we tend to see as criminal intent. It's a handicap to an investigator and one I find having you on the team helps me avoid."

"It's kind of you to say so, Inspector," Pauline said. "Now, where was I? Oh, yes. Once again, I was shown as having been on the wrong trail and you were being criticized by your colleagues and superiors, Inspector."

He shrugged and dismissed the thought with a wave of his hand. "I'm used to it."

"It was at this point I decided that solving the mystery of who hit Harry Common might unlock this puzzle."

"And that's where the link to those 'poverty activists' came in again," Theresa said.

Pauline nodded. "I thought if I followed that, I might get information tying Harry to the poverty activists or maybe even the nationalists." She paused and addressed Alf and his group. "At times, I thought you nationalists more likely; politics is such an ugly business when people lose sight of their purpose. The links however led me back to the poverty activists, whose cause seemed so much kinder but whose manner seemed so much worse."

"No one goes into politics for honest reasons, Miss Riddell, as I've told you before," Ramsay said. "Scratch their claims and you'll find self-interest is just below the skin."

Pauline smiled. "I'm not ready to go quite that far, Inspector, but too many more cases like this and I fear I will."

"You didn't think the extortion demands worth your attention?" Theresa asked.

"The police kept those close to their chests, I'm afraid. I knew nothing about them until just before Paisley was captured. I would have liked to look into that, but the police were working on it, and they would've been angry to find me snooping around in their patch," Pauline said.

"You can be sure of it," Ramsay said, grinning.

"It was my interview with Sir Robert that gave me the clue," Pauline said. "Something he said. His anger at the death of Harry Common was understandable; they'd known each other many years and while not close friends, Sir Robert clearly had a lot of respect for Harry. He said, 'Harry was a good man who could be trusted to do the right thing.' At the time, I took that as a general statement but I began to think it was more pointed, more real."

"It sounds like the sort of thing we say about someone who's died," Theresa said, "rather than a clue."

Pauline nodded. "As I said, that's what I thought. Then I wondered if it meant something specific and if that something was what led to his death, though I don't think the intention was to murder him."

"The police doctor agrees with you, Miss Riddell," Ramsay said. "He doubts even Harry Common knew he had developed a weakness in his bones. It was early in his illness."

"He was ill?" Theresa asked.

"He had something called Paget's Disease," Pauline replied.

"What's that?" Theresa asked.

"It's a disease where the bones become brittle and easily broken," Ramsay said. "In this case, it was Harry Common's skull that was so seriously weakened by the disease that a punch could shatter it. He died almost immediately."

"Poor man," Theresa said sadly.

"Yes," Pauline said. "Poor man. But he probably didn't know, and he died mercifully quickly. He wouldn't suffer."

"I feel sorry even for the man who hit him," Theresa said. "He must be devastated. Thinking a simple bout of fisticuffs had led to a man's death."

"I feel little sympathy for him," Ramsay said. "He attacked Common with ugly motives. Even if he didn't mean to kill him, he had murder in his heart."

"I don't understand," Theresa said. "Wasn't this just a pub quarrel gone wrong?"

Pauline shook her head. "No. It was much worse. The so-called poverty activists had tricked Harry into making a fake, look-alike Gospel carrying case so they could substitute the two. They told Harry it was to be a joke, a lunchbox that looked like a briefcase, you see. He probably saw through that when he was told what it must look like, or maybe only when he saw a newspaper photo of the security guards carrying the Gospels' case. When they discovered the switch, they thought Harry had double-crossed them and set their man Gently on him."

"Poor Harry," Theresa repeated. "How did they get into the bank though?"

"They leaned on the bank's under-manager to let them into the vault," Pauline said. "Their plan was to ransom the Gospels and pocket the cash. After all, no one would know where the money was to be spent if it was being shared out among the poor. They, of course, considered themselves poor and therefore worthy beneficiaries."

"And that part of their plan seemed to be working well for them," Ramsay said. "Until they opened the case."

"But who could they sell them to?" Alf asked, suddenly breaking into the conversation. "After all, they couldn't just sell the Gospels on the open market."

"Here's where I'm guessing," Pauline said. "I think it was Warkworth who planned the whole enterprise. One of Warkworth's companies is also in the metals business and he knew Croker and he knew Graystoke as an art dealer. He knew Temperley as the metalworker's union man and that set the ball rolling."

"Why include Graystoke?" Theresa asked. "He doesn't seem to be necessary."

"He was supposed to be the cut-out," Pauline said. "Warkworth had one of his men set it up with Graystoke as the supposed head of the operation. Graystoke knew, or maybe learned, the man was one of Warkworth's men but went along with it. I imagine he thought the opportunity for blackmail in future years would be very lucrative. It was also why Warkworth gave me the Purcell Gallery's name as a possibly crooked dealer. He was pointing me away from Graystoke, you see."

"What nice people," Elsie said, grimacing.

"Their biggest mistake was Temperley selecting Harry Common to make the false carrying case. Harry was a good choice being as he was a superior craftsman, but he was also someone who loved antiquities and didn't want this treasure hidden away in a millionaire's private collection. As Sir Robert said, you could trust Harry to do the right thing."

"Hmm," Ramsay said. "The right thing in my mind would have been to alert the police."

"Then the Gospels would have returned to London," Pauline continued, "and Harry saw a way to correct this ancient wrong. And this is where I shall hand over to Inspector Ramsay because it is very much the police's story from here."

"Miss Riddell means I can tell you the final results of the Task Force's work, which I can as the government has published their own report to satisfy the public a full investigation was carried out."

"That's exactly what I mean, Inspector," Pauline said. She wasn't prepared to take an active part in repeating the published document as it bore so little resemblance to the truth.

"Based on the evidence Miss Riddell provided, and our own evidence, the investigation concluded Harry double-crossed Temperley, perhaps with the intention of alerting the police and having Temperley arrested with the false case. We can't know because he was killed soon after. At any rate, the attempt to steal the Gospels failed, thankfully, and we still have such a treasure available for the people to admire."

"What puzzles me, Inspector, is why Warkworth wasn't arrested," Alf said.

Ramsay shook his head. "No evidence, I'm afraid." He looked around the waiting faces, expecting questions.

When none came, he continued, "All should have gone well for Harry, he could have had time to carry out whatever plan he had in mind, but one of the gang actually wanted to see the Gospels. Harry was probably relying on them being so uninterested in the Gospels, this wouldn't happen. Sadly, it did. They broke open the carrying case they had and found it empty."

"They decided Harry Common had switched the cases between the vault and handing it over to Temperley. They attacked him, with disastrous results for Harry," Pauline added.

"Why involve Harry in the robbery at all?" Alf asked.

"We think it was insurance," Pauline said. "If the case wasn't incriminating enough to keep him silent then having Harry take it from the vault meant he was in too deep to rat on them."

"I suspect they made it impossible for Harry to refuse," Ramsay said. "His mother's safety would be a strong lever to use."

"If Harry had switched the cases, wouldn't they look for Harry's accomplices?" Theresa asked. "The under-manager, for instance. He must have seen Harry switch the cases, if he was in the vault with him waiting to lock up."

"Maybe not," Ramsay said. "We don't know what went on in there, after all. He must have persuaded them he didn't see the switch, or they would have started with him. I suspect they would have come back to him if we hadn't gotten on their trail so quickly."

"They didn't know Harry had any accomplices, is how I see it," Pauline replied. "They did search Harry's house, his garden shed, and everywhere they thought he might have hidden the Gospels. His mother had only just finished cleaning up the house when I arrived to interview her."

"So, there were three mysteries to be solved here," Theresa said, thoughtfully. "The bank robbery for money, the death of Harry Common, and the attempted theft of the Lindisfarne Gospels?"

"Unfortunately," Ramsay said, "the bank robbery for money was too soon written off as a genuine robbery and handed back to the local police. Similarly, the death of Harry Common was considered just a drunken brawl gone horribly wrong, also handed over to the local police."

"You're being too censorious of the Scotland Yard man, Inspector," Pauline said, smiling at Ramsay's northern prejudice against southerners. "The team did keep in contact with the local police, you told me."

Ramsay nodded. "We did but the three strands should have been working together."

"I'm pleased they weren't," Pauline said. "It meant I could snoop around and that helped me see the links."

"Was the other robbery really a diversion from the Gospels robbery?"

"It was," Pauline said. "Though not working directly with the Gospels thieves."

"I don't understand," Theresa said. "Were they, or weren't they?"

"The bank robbery gang were organized to carry out their planned raid on the night a big local employer's payroll came in. The Gospel gang knew this and organized their theft for the same night. The Gospel gang knew; the bank robbery gang didn't."

"Even if they had known," Theresa said, "from the money robbers' point of view, it would be a good idea, having another theft happening at the same time, I mean. It would confuse the investigation."

"It would have been, but the money robbers say they didn't know of the Gospel robbery, and I believe them," Ramsay said. "Of course, we can't know for sure they didn't but it's certain the Gospel gang knew of the other robbery and coordinated their theft to take advantage."

"The money robbery had to take place on Thursday night because that's when the payroll for the town's biggest factory came in. It's all dispersed to the workers on Friday, you see."

"Yes, I see that," Theresa said, thoughtfully. "We often had these kinds of scheduling opportunities in the war."

Pauline laughed. "The men who planned this one didn't serve in the war. Their occupations made them exempt. Still, they can and did plan and execute their theft very competently."

"Just not for a good cause," Ramsay said grimly.

"My short experience of investigating leads me to suspect they felt the cause was more than justified, Inspector," Pauline said. "People can convince themselves they are deserving victims of something or other without turning a hair. Your good cause may not be mine and vice versa."

"Stealing is never right, Miss Riddell," Ramsay said, grinning. "Even my cynicism doesn't go that far."

"I'm with you, Inspector, about stealing," Pauline said. "It's just I've recently seen how easily ordinary people justify even their worst actions and think they're the good people in every circumstance."

"One day you'll move to my opinion, Miss Riddell. Only bad people rationalize their behavior as good. But they do know it's wrong, believe me."

"In this case," Theresa said. "They decided they were

231

the poor who needed to be made rich. They don't appear to have had any intention of sharing it with anyone else."

"Nor did they," Ramsay said, "though they claim they did."

"You should explain more about Harry's death, Inspector," Pauline said. "That success was more your finding than mine."

"It was you who made the connection to the gang and to Sir Robert," Ramsay said. "Without that, it would have remained an unfortunate but coincidental death."

"But you had to believe in the connection, Inspector, when your colleagues didn't."

"Very well," Ramsay said. "As Miss Riddell said earlier, Harry Common's death looked like an unfortunate accident and nothing to do with the thefts. It happened the day after the thefts and he was a man who, so far as any of us knew, wasn't involved with any of the suspects."

"Then the leader of the poverty group told me Harry was a member of the metalworker's union," Pauline said, quite forgetting she'd asked Ramsay to explain.

"Which," Ramsay said, with emphasis, "isn't at all unusual here where we have factories, mines, and shipyards on every corner. Again, it didn't seem a close enough link."

"Quite so," Pauline said, smiling at Ramsay's forceful resumption of his narrative.

"Then Miss Riddell's talk with Sir Robert, a character we hadn't come across in our sweep of suspects, because he wasn't one, identified Sir Robert as someone who might want to own the Gospels. When she shared this information with me, I thought this significant enough to warrant closer inspection."

"That's when you discovered the man who hit Harry Common was one of the gangs?" Theresa asked.

"Yes. Originally, Harry's death seemed to have no links to the bank robbery or the attempt to steal the Gospels. Miss Riddell found a connection. He had friends among the poverty activist gang but so do many, many others."

"And that was enough to change your mind?"

"Miss Riddell found people who'd seen him wearing large, heavy metal rings. Naturally, he'd removed them before the police arrived on the night of Harry's death, but we found them in his house. He hadn't wanted to get rid of them, you see. One ring matched a cut on Harry's face."

"I still don't see why he would want to assault Harry if he wasn't part of the plan," Alf said.

"Temperley knew him," Ramsay said. "And knew he was someone who liked violence and always needed money."

"It was risky though," Theresa said. "Harry may have won a straightforward fight. What could have induced this man Gently to take such a chance?"

"Harry was unlikely to win even if he'd been healthy," Ramsay said. "Gently had been a local boxer with many fights to his name. And his inducement was also pressing. Like Paisley, he had gambling debts and some unpleasant people after him."

"They can't have meant to kill Harry, though," Alf said. "They'd never find the Gospels without Harry."

Ramsay nodded. "The idea was to beat Harry until he agreed to hand over the Gospels. Remember, Temperley and his gang didn't know what Harry had done with the Gospels. They thought Harry had gone into business for himself with a view to taking all the money."

"I imagine they were furious," Pauline said. "A comrade stealing from them. The worst kind of betrayal, in their minds."

"But why did Harry do it?" Theresa asked. "Surely, he would realize the gang would come after him when the switch was discovered?"

Ramsay nodded. "Temperley said Common had told them there must be a number of decoys in different banks and what they'd stolen must have been one of them."

"But they stole it from the vault," Theresa said, "where presumably only the real one would be kept."

Pauline nodded. "Harry had thought of that and told them the newspapers and radio must have been fed the false information and the real Gospels must be in another bank's vault."

"They didn't believe him?" Theresa asked

"Temperley said they couldn't be sure," Ramsay said. "Which is why he sent Gently to find out. Unfortunately, Harry died instantly and they learned nothing."

"Inspector," Alf said, "how much were they expecting to get from the theft?"

"Graystoke says he was told they would share one hundred thousand pounds between them. With Graystoke being the one to share the money. The Martin's bank robbers got away with fifty thousand, so you can see how much Warkworth wanted the Gospels."

"Phew," Alf said. "I suppose when they found they didn't have the Gospels, that's when they decided to ask for a ransom?"

Ramsay nodded.

"How much was that?" Alf asked.

"They wanted a quarter of a million," Ramsay said.

"They wouldn't have got that, surely, Inspector?" Theresa said.

"Even if it was negotiated down, it would still be far more than the weekly payroll of even the biggest factories here," Ramsay said. "It would be many times as much as a bank robbery and well worth killing for. People could live a life of ease most places around the world on that."

"Still, it's a leap of faith," Theresa said. "Imagining they could get that much and not hand over the valuables in return."

"I'm a believer in faith," Pauline said, "and they must have thought it was worth a try. After all, if they didn't, they had nothing to show for the risks they'd taken."

"It seems to me, had they just shut up at this point, they would have been safe."

Pauline said. "If it had just been the attempted theft of the Gospels, yes. But they'd killed Harry Common. Once the police arrested Gently it was always going to be a race to get some money from the enterprise before the police got them."

"What a tangled web," Theresa said. "Poverty activists who were only interested in enriching themselves, a man who made the false carrying cases who was pretending to work for them but was actually working against them, people who thought the Gospels should be here and not in a museum in London setting the whole sorry train of events in motion and getting nothing for their pains. And then it all unraveled like a woolen jumper with a hole in it."

"Sadly," Ramsay said, "someone had to die to unravel it. I wish it weren't so."

Pauline nodded. "I do too. Harry Common seemed to be a good man. I feel his role in the affair would have turned out to be a heroic one if Sir Robert is to be believed. But we shall never know for certain."

"All's well that ends well, they say," Theresa said. "And for you, Miss Riddell, it seems like another success to add to your earlier ones. Or so this morning's paper says."

"Poppy again," Pauline said, smiling at Ramsay. "She may have fallen out with us but she's still recording our careers."

"When she phoned and asked for a quote last night, something she could use in her article," Ramsay said, "she told me she'd be leaving for London very soon. Did she tell you?"

Pauline shook her head. "She hasn't been in touch. I fear Poppy feels I betrayed her. After all she's done for me, that hurt her a lot."

"Did she do it for you, Miss Riddell?" Ramsay asked. "Or did she ride to the top on your coattails?"

"It depends on where you view it from, Inspector. I never wanted her to write any of it and tried to moderate what she did write. She always told me I didn't understand journalism."

"And what did you say to that, Pauline?" Theresa asked.

"Nothing. What could I say? The truth is I understood journalism very clearly and that's why I didn't want any of my actions written about, even by someone I thought was a friend."

"Welcome to my world, Miss Riddell," Ramsay said. "You're very young to see the news so clearly. I'm surprised, though maybe I shouldn't be."

"I've read the newspapers since I was very young," Pauline said. "Over the years, there were incidents in our local neighborhood that I had some actual knowledge of and what the newspaper reports said bore no resemblance to the actual events."

"Well, I hope you and your friend can find a way to forgive each other," Theresa said. "We need all the friends we can get in this vale of tears."

"Amen to that," Pauline said, smiling. "What say you, Inspector?"

"I say you should do what's best for you, Miss Riddell," Ramsay said. "If that is forgiving Poppy, then do that. If it's move on with your life, don't be held back by feeling something is your duty and yours alone."

"And look forward to our next case?"

"Certainly, which I hope won't involve anyone getting themselves killed," Ramsay said.

"This would have been a very dull case without the death," Pauline reminded him.

Ramsay smiled but it was a sad expression; there was little humor in it. "Dull and boring are the highest praise I can heap upon my investigations. I like those words for it means no one was really hurt."

Pauline shook her head. "In my mind, it means the cases meant nothing to anyone. Hurt means passion and we all need something in our lives to be passionate about otherwise we're just born and then die with nothing but work in between. There must be more than that to life, surely." She looked at Theresa who was almost as somber as Ramsay.

"I'm afraid I agree with the Inspector, Pauline," Theresa said. "I saw much passion in the war and all of it leading to horrific results. We Catholics speak about passion a lot in our liturgy, and I'm always troubled by it."

Seeing the two weren't going to be persuaded and acknowledging even her own experience spoke against her, Pauline said, "I accept your arguments, but human nature won't change. Passions will always be roused, and terrible things will be done, which means we must do everything we can to right the wrongs and I intend to continue doing that, come what may."

"Oh, I think Inspector Ramsay and I agree we should

contend against our human failings, Pauline," Theresa said, "only that we wish it weren't so."

Feeling a change of subject was in order, Ramsay said, "And to ensure you always have some windmill at which to tilt, Miss Riddell, I shall call on your assistance when the next intriguing case comes along."

"I hope it may be soon, Inspector," Pauline said. "I have an empty space in my life that these puzzles help me fill."

Chapter Thirty-Four

A SERIOUS MORAL

AS PAULINE and Ramsay walked back to his car, Ramsay said, "I hope in that empty space you find room for your friend Poppy. I know she didn't behave well on this occasion, but I feel she will have need of all the friends she can get."

Pauline paused, trying to explain what she wanted to say. Finally, she began, "Have you heard that song, *I Know an old Lady Who Swallowed a Fly*, Inspector?"

He shook his head. "I can't say I have, Miss Riddell. Why?"

"It's a silly song, quite popular now, with a serious message," Pauline replied, "and it sums up my feelings toward Poppy perfectly."

He laughed. "You'll have to explain."

"In the song, an old lady swallows a fly and thinks perhaps she'll die. So, she swallows a spider to catch the fly, but it wriggles and tickles inside her, so she swallows a bird to catch the spider, then a cat to catch the bird, then a dog to catch the cat, then a cow to catch the dog, and then a horse – and then she's dead, of course."

"It sounds ridiculous," Ramsay agreed. "Where does Poppy come into this?"

"It is a silly song, but it has a serious moral to teach: Don't turn small, harmless problems into huge, life-ending events."

"Yes, I see that."

"Well, Poppy and the media in general are like that old lady. They take small, usually local events and turn them into global catastrophes."

"I know what you mean, but it's how they make their living, Miss Riddell."

"Their living is creating mayhem for individuals, as well as nations. I don't want that in my life anymore. I may not be able to stop reporters turning small border disputes into a World War, but I can stop them hammering on my door day and night with impertinent, offensive questions and comments. And I can do that starting with Poppy."

"I do understand how you feel now, Miss Riddell," Ramsay said. "I just hope that sometime soon you'll forgive Poppy for she needs you, whether she knows it or not."

"I'll try, Inspector," Pauline said. "Just now, I can't."

Chapter Thirty-Five

SOMETIME LATER

SIR ROBERT LAURISTON knocked on the bank's solid wooden door, made when banks were rich enough to signal their strength in the branches they built. After a few moments, when he knew he was being scrutinized from inside, the door opened.

"Come in, Robert," the manager said, stepping aside to let Sir Robert enter. "Punctual as ever." He grinned as his guest passed by on his way to the manager's office.

"You know me," Sir Robert said, looking back to see the door once again being locked.

"I thought you may get stuck in the rush hour traffic," the manager said, leading Sir Robert into his office. "Sherry or whisky?"

"Do you still have that old Glenfiddich?"

"I do," the manager said, opening his desk side drawer and extracting the bottle. Two glasses followed and the two friends quietly toasted 'absent, fallen comrades' before sitting to enjoy the mellow single malt in companionable silence for a few minutes.

"Have you seen any signs of surveillance?" Sir Robert finally asked.

The manager shook his head. "None. Though I think it too soon to be sure it's safe."

"Yet we can't leave it too long," Sir Robert said. "One day, it will be open for all to see but until then the people in London will want it back. Their story about an attempt to steal the Gospels may satisfy the public and save face all around, but they'll be searching for it, you can be sure. It belongs here in the north, and it will remain here in safety."

"Shall we?" Mitchell gestured to the door.

"Yes, but we leave our drinks here," Sir Robert said. "It would be easy to spill a drink and I won't have the book coming to harm at our hands."

They rose and the manager led the way out of his office and down the stairs leading to the vault.

"They won't let any other treasures come back here again, you can be sure of that," Mitchell said as he opened the vault's steel-barred door.

"Perhaps not," Sir Robert said. "One day, though, they'll have no choice. People will have what's theirs by right."

They stepped inside the vault and the manager closed the door behind them. He opened another door leading into a room where the walls were covered in safety deposit boxes.

"The copy. Was it good?" Mitchell asked. "I didn't get to see it."

"Very good," Sir Robert replied. "I couldn't tell them apart. The British Museum's craftsmen are the best around. The public is losing nothing by seeing an imitation rather than the original."

"Maybe they always have seen a copy," the manager

said. "Maybe the copy is what's on display and the original is kept in a vault. After all, people only file past the exhibits giving each no more than a cursory glance. The public would never have known."

Sir Robert nodded as he unlocked the door to his safety deposit box and lifted the box out. He placed it on the table that ran along the center of the room and opened the lid.

"You're probably right," he said. "After all, keeping parchment over a thousand years old in good order is a difficult task, which, I imagine, is why they had the copy ready to send up here immediately after the original went missing."

"Are you sure it is the original? You said yourself you couldn't tell them apart."

"I'm sure," Sir Robert replied. "I hear, from friends, there's much concern among the great and good over what has happened. It may just be a smokescreen, but I think not. They really are upset. The Government has been informed."

"That is a sign of seriousness," the manager said thoughtfully. "Can we northerners expect reprisals? You know the sort of thing – no one leaves the classroom until someone snitches on the paper-plane thrower?"

"Possibly but it will be done in the most secret of ways," Sir Robert said, lifting the book from the box with his gloved hands. He placed it on the table and gently opened the book. In the garish overhead lights, the colors of the illustrated capitals glowed as they might have done in candlelight when the color was still wet.

The two men gazed at the book in silent awe. "When can northern people see it? That's the question," the manager said.

"When we have a government here to take charge of

it," Sir Robert replied. "I won't have it displayed to artistic dilettantes or the self-proclaimed worthy few. This is the heritage of everyone from the north and it is for them first and foremost. Others will be able to see it as well, of course. It's a treasure from England's past and it should be shared."

"What if self-government never comes?"

"Then at some appropriate time, long after they've forgotten this embarrassing event, we will exchange the real for the fake. Knowing the experts, it will take them a decade to notice and a further decade to stop arguing about the switch and who did it."

"By which time we'll be gone?"

"I would think so, wouldn't you?" Sir Robert asked. "I plan to keep pushing for devolved government to my dying day so it will be late in my life when I come to understand it isn't going to happen."

"Have your friends given any suggestion as to who the powers that be think has the original?"

"They haven't. I imagine everyone has suspicions and I imagine some will suspect me but there's nothing to link me with what happened. I think we're safe, though I urge you to keep your eyes open. They may be watching the bank."

"Wouldn't they more likely watch your home?"

"I'm keeping a close watch there, too," Sir Robert said. "Up to now, there's no sign of anyone watching my house. Though I thought there might be."

"What about that young woman detective?"

"Miss Riddell? Oh, I think she knows, which is why I thought we might have been under surveillance."

"If we're not, maybe she doesn't know? I hope not anyway. It makes me uncomfortable."

"Perhaps, you're right," Sir Robert said soothingly. "Perhaps I thought her more knowing than she was."

"It's nearly a month now," the manager said. "If she had told anyone, we'd have known about it."

Sir Robert nodded. "Unless she agrees with our cause."

"She seemed a very honest young woman," the manager said. "Would she really keep quiet, even if she did support our cause?"

Sir Robert returned the book to the safety deposit box and closed the lid. "Sometimes even the most patriotic of people see an opposing cause they think warrants support. I'm reminded of George Washington's comment about Lord Howe. He said, 'Either that gentleman doesn't know his business or he's on our side' or something like that. Of course, Lord Howe knew the soldiering business and we'll never really know if he'd decided the rebels' cause was worthy of support. We can only surmise. As in this present case with Miss Riddell."

He returned the box into the opening and locked the door on it. "Sadly," he continued, "I can't come and see this every day. I wish I could but continually opening it would increase the possible damage. In darkness and sealed tight, it will keep for many years to come."

"Maybe, but when can it be moved?" the manager asked. "Officially, I don't know what's in any safety deposit box, but it would still go badly for me if it's found here."

"If we see no surveillance for two more weeks, I'll take it to my controlled cabinet. It will be safe there for decades, though I hope it will be on display long before then."

"My other concern," the manager said, "is they realize the Gospels never left our vault. Then they'll realize that if Frank showed Harry to the deposit box, the switch must have happened before then, which will point to me."

"The authorities know Frank let Harry in," Sir Robert said, "because Temperley told them. He also told them he didn't enter the bank. He only took the case from Harry, which is why they thought Harry was the one who double-crossed them."

"Then you can be sure the police will keep watching," Mitchell said.

Lauriston nodded. His expression serious. "Yes, but they must be careful. The authorities have published a story that makes them and the public happy. They can't upset that now."

"And how will you give it back if self-rule never comes, without telling them you have it?"

Sir Robert laughed. "I'll create an event and ask for a copy of the Gospels to put on display during it, of course. They can hardly refuse that."

"That's true," the manager said, as he locked the doors behind them. "Then, at the end, you'll send the original back to them, very clever."

They returned to the office and finished their drinks in companionable silence.

Next in the Miss Riddell Cozy Mysteries series

vinci-books.com/murderforchristmas

A forged will, a brutal murder, and a family in danger: Miss Riddell must unravel a web of deceit and murder to save her family.

Miss Riddell definitely isn't having a merry Christmas. With her mother sick and brother pestering her to investigate a forged will, the worst winter in decades has her longing to return to regular life. And just as a series of ugly incidents in the village pushes the pressure to a boiling point, things take a deadly turn when her cousin is brutally murdered.

Turn the page for a free preview...

A Murder for Christmas: Chapter One

FAMILY MATTERS

North Riding of Yorkshire - December 21, 1962

"You have to, Sis," Alan said, "I said you would."

"Why did you do that?" Pauline demanded angrily. Alan was the last word in obnoxious older brothers. Even as a kid, he was forever getting his younger siblings in trouble with one lunatic scheme after another. Weren't the older kids supposed to be more mature than the younger ones? Pauline was sure there was a popular expression to that effect.

"It will be easy for you," Alan said. "Look at how you're always solving murders and such for the police. This is simple compared to that. Some small local disturbances are all we're asking you to solve. It will take you a matter of hours. It won't even disturb your holiday."

Her holiday. Two weeks with Mum and Dad on the farm over a cold and increasingly snowy Christmas, with Mum ill and Dad laid up. Some holiday! Now this idiot, her blasted brother, had promised her time looking into silly pranks in his village five miles away. With the roads the way they were and the weather the way it was, how could she do that without moving in with Alan and his wife, Bessie?

"I'm not doing it, Alan. Mum and dad need me here, not over at Goathland, chasing naughty children."

"Me and Jim will come to the farm every day to look after the beasts," Alan said, "and you'll have it all sorted out in a day, likely."

This was ridiculous. She'd driven down to her family home only the night before, straight after work, taking this Saturday morning off work to be here earlier. It had been a frightening journey with snow on the roads here in the Dales. On the high ground, a wicked wind swirled the snow in the headlamps, blinding her view through the icy wind-screen. And there'd been few other cars on the road after she'd left the main highway. Now, next morning, when she was barely recovered from her fright, Alan arrives at the farm demanding she leave and solve mysterious events in the village and farms around him.

"No," Pauline said. "You people live there; it will be your children doing this. You local folk sort it out yourselves."

"It's not the children, Polly," Alan said, lapsing into the family nickname Pauline hated. "We thought that too at first. But it isn't. It's something bigger than it seems."

"In Goathland! What could be *big* in any way in Goathland?"

As she followed him back to his farm, however, she remembered what could be bigger. She couldn't miss it, or to be precise, them. Stark opal white against low black clouds that threatened yet more snow, the giant 'golf balls' of the Fylingdales early warning station loomed menacingly over moor and dale. Placed there by the United States Air

Force and operated by the Royal Air Force, they were supposed to give the West fifteen minutes warning should the Soviet Union launch its intercontinental nuclear ballistic missiles, or so it was said. No one knew for sure. They were too secret for real knowledge. Pauline frowned as she tried to keep her eyes on the road and away from the golf balls. Her first investigation (she never said 'case' it was too official-sounding) had been about spies, though she hadn't realized that until the very end. Was this about spies too and should she be thinking about them from the very beginning?

After saying hello to Alan's wife, Bessie, and the children, Alan said, "We're going straight to the manor house."

"Why?" Pauline asked, bewildered. The family at the manor hadn't been mentioned in Alan's earlier list of odd incidents.

"Because they have a story to tell I think you should hear."

Leaving her own car in the yard of Alan's farm, Pauline climbed into his Land Rover and they set off back up the farm road to the country lane that connected the farms along this dale with the outside world.

"What's this all about, Alan?" Pauline asked, as she pulled her coat, scarf, and collar closer around her. The Land Rover's heating was making no impression on the air temperature inside the cab, not that Alan seemed to notice. She wished she offered to drive in her own comfortable Wolseley, with its better seats and heating.

"Mr. Thornton will explain," he said.

"What has it to do with the incidents you told me about?"

"Not sure. Maybe nothing. I think it does but you'll have to decide for yourself."

Pauline gritted her teeth and stared out of the window.

The afternoon looked like it promised more snow by the time they were returning home. Maybe the Land Rover with its four-wheel drive was the better choice for this journey. As it bumped over the frozen, rutted farm road, however, jarring every bone in her body, she found that little comfort. And imagining the drive back to her parents' farm through snow-covered roads in her own car gave her the shudders.

At the manor, an old-fashioned stone-built house that hadn't been upgraded in any of the architectural styles of the past four hundred years (and was all the better for it, in Pauline's opinion) she met Frank Thornton, the soon-to-be lord of the manor. Or at least that was what had been expected until the family solicitor had hurried up to the manor on the death of Frank's father only two days ago with some disastrous news.

"So, you see, Miss Riddell," Frank Thornton said, "we're in a pickle."

"Let me get this clear in my mind," Pauline said. "Your father has been training you up to take over the estate all your life. He never suggested any other course of action was being considered?"

"That's correct."

"The will has been lodged with the family solicitors for decades, since your older brother was killed in World War II, in fact? No one else has had access to it?" Pauline asked, with growing incredulity.

"That's correct," Thornton agreed.

"And the will, so far as everyone understood, named you as the heir to the estate and your younger brother, Anthony, would have had an annual remittance?"

"That's correct."

"But when your father died, the solicitor drew the will

from the safe, preparing to bring it to read out after the funeral and found that it named Anthony as heir and gave you a single bequest of five hundred pounds?" Pauline was beginning to think she was an actor in a stage farce.

"That's it."

"Then the solicitor called you and suggested holding off reading the will until an investigation could be made."

"Yes, and the police came, listened to what we had to say and took the will to check for fingerprints and for forged signatures," Frank Thornton said. "That's when the real nightmare began."

Pauline nodded, and said, "Because they've done that now and say it's in order. The signature is your father's and the will is genuine."

"Exactly. The will, they say, looks genuine enough and it stands," Thornton said.

"Aye," Alan said, breaking in on the tale, "but the difficulty is Tony Thornton wants to sell the land to the highest bidder, developers to be precise."

Pauline looked at Frank Thornton for confirmation.

He nodded. "My brother is a man who likes his life in London, Paris, St. Tropez and all those places the rich and idle go. Only, he can't really afford it on his present income. This lovely old estate and all the farms will be gone in a heartbeat, if this will stands, for he'll sell to the highest bidder."

"You're quite sure your father didn't change the will?" she asked, looking him squarely in the eye.

"I'm sure he did not," Thornton replied, "and so is our solicitor. He's as distraught over this as we all are. Somehow the will was changed and we have to prove it."

"You and your solicitor do realize, I suppose, that the

253

only people who could have altered the will must work in the solicitor's office?"

Thornton hesitated before saying, "Naturally, we thought of that, but it isn't possible. John Ogilvie, his father, and his grandfather have been the Thornton family solicitors for almost a century. They hold that position of trust because they are eminently trustworthy. It is impossible to imagine anyone in their office doing such a thing."

"How else could it be done, then?" Pauline said, now fully incredulous of the blind, willful obstinacy of such a statement.

"Alan says you have found many amazing solutions to problems before. Indeed, even I have heard of your successes. We hope you will be able to show how this was done and exonerate the Ogilvies of any wrongdoing."

"This is a matter for the police," Pauline said.

"The police have already stated that the will is genuine and there's no case to be investigated. Indeed, they practically accused me of trying to overturn it because I was upset at being cut out."

"If the will is genuine, as their experts proved, then that is the only conclusion to be drawn," Pauline said. She held up her hand to prevent the angry outburst she could see about to begin, and continued, "If the will is false, as you and the lawyer say, then it can only have been falsified in the solicitor's office. Unless they can show it was elsewhere at some time and they failed to check it hadn't been tampered with while outside their care, which isn't much of an improvement in their culpability, frankly."

"I don't like the tone of this," Thornton said. "Alan said you could help us but all I'm hearing is slanderous remarks about an honest man and his family's firm."

Pauline shook her head. "Then get a private investigator

who will pander to your sensitivities. The answer to this will be bad for someone and pretending that it isn't one of the Thornton or Ogilvie families won't help you."

Frank Thornton's expression was thunderous but, with a visible effort, he said, "I thought you were a private investigator."

"I investigate puzzles privately and people do pay me for assisting them but I'm not in the business of being a private investigator. I take cases where people want the truth and, where appropriate, justice. Neither of these things appear to be wanted here."

"That's not true. Everyone here knows my father's wishes and this will doesn't reflect those wishes. He would never have left the estate to Tony who is a scoundrel and a leech. Our father knew exactly what would happen to the estate he loved if it should ever fall into Tony's hands."

That gave Pauline a thought. "Could this be simply a prank by your brother? Knowing how you and your father thought of him, could he have substituted the will just to make mischief?"

"This is no prank, Miss Riddell," Thornton said. "My brother outruns his allowance every month and is constantly asking me for more money. He's sold almost everything that had been handed down to him that he could sell. This is the act of a desperate man who intends to ruin dozens of lives in order to keep enjoying a life far beyond his means."

"What did he have handed down to him?"

"He had the bulk of our mother's funds," Thornton said. "It was understood that I, as the first born, would have the estate and so he got the bulk of mother's money. He has spent it all, thousands of pounds wasted on drink, drugs and, well, let's say parties."

"What Mr. Thornton says is true, Pauline," Alan said.

"Everyone hereabouts will vouch for that. Last time he came up here, two years ago now, the goings on at the Dower house scandalized the whole neighborhood. He still has the old Dower house, you see."

"Mr. Thornton, I understand your feelings and," Pauline said, "those of your tenants and the village at large but, I repeat, if you want to know the truth of this, you must allow an investigator to expose whoever has done this, even if it is someone inside your household or the Ogilvie law office. There can be no other way."

"I refuse to believe it is anyone we know or have known these past years," Thornton said.

"Then you should have no reason to refuse to have a proper investigation. Indeed, when you've thought about it further, you'll see that by not investigating properly you leave suspicion hanging over your household and the Ogilvie office. Would Mr. Ogilvie be against a thorough investigation?"

"I don't know."

"Shouldn't we ask him?"

Thornton frowned as he struggled with the idea of calling the family's loyal solicitors and suggesting such a thing while desperate for an answer that made sense before the estate and its people were destroyed.

"I will phone John and do my best to suggest it without destroying their confidence in me," he said at last.

"Their confidence in you? They work for you," Pauline said. Her years of dealing with boardroom quarrels, and the board's conflicts with suppliers, was outraged by the antiquated notions his speech suggested.

"Miss Riddell," Thornton said, "in the world where you work, that may be considered a sharp thing to say but here in the real world we value mutual relationships. It's true we pay them for specific services but in return they provide wide loyalty and support when we need it."

Pauline shrugged. "Do, or say, what you need to make it happen. If Mr. Ogilvie can't accept a fair investigation into how the will was switched, you may as well start packing now."

Thornton nodded and left the room abruptly.

Pauline looked at Alan questioningly.

"He'll call from the estate office," Alan said. "He won't be a moment."

"I hope not. I want to get back to mother. She needs me more than any of you do."

"Mother has a bad cold, Pauline. I and all the others here will lose our livelihoods and Mr. Thornton his whole estate."

"Mother has flu," Pauline said, "and people her age die from flu. You folks can find other investigators, but you want me to do it for free and in my two weeks annual holiday instead of looking after Mum and Dad."

Fortunately, before the argument grew worse, Frank Thornton returned. His expression was lighter than when he'd left.

"John Ogilvie would be happy to speak to you," he said. "He's frantic to find the original will and recover the damage his office appears to have done. He'll be at his office for the rest of the day if you will drop by."

A Murder for Christmas: Chapter Two

A HOPELESS TASK

Looking out from Alan's Land Rover on the way into the village, Pauline watched the snow, still thin but falling steadily, piling up at the roadside and in the fields, where the wind was shaping it into drifts. *We should be going back to our parents' farm at Troutsdale,* she thought, *not further away from it.*

"John Ogilvie is a good man," Alan said suddenly, breaking into her thoughts.

"I've no doubt," Pauline said, "but if that will is a forgery then it happened in his office and you got me involved with it under false pretences."

"I did not," Alan exclaimed, "the will is linked to the incidents."

"Poppycock," Pauline snapped. "You knew I'd give in on the incidents because they were harming ordinary people but you thought I'd never waste time on the landed gentry."

"I thought nothing of the sort," Alan replied, equally angry. "Don't you see? This is just the latest in these incidents and as nasty as the others."

"There's nothing 'latest' about this at all. The forgery happened years ago and came to light now, coincidentally around the time of these admittedly unpleasant crimes."

"You don't know that. You only believe it," Alan said, "and in case you hadn't taken it properly into your elevated thinking, the will harms dozens of ordinary people and only one 'landed gentry', using your ugly term."

"Aren't the Thorntons landed gentry then?"

"Frank Thornton and his father before him are decent, hard-working people, not idle loafers, which is what that term implies. But, even if they weren't, the people who will be really hurt here are me, Bessie and our children and the two other tenant farmers of the Thornton estate. And they have families too."

Pauline nodded and sighed. "You're right, of course, it is always ordinary people who suffer in upheavals but I still say you've tricked me into investigating this will."

They drove on in silence until the lights of Goathland, lit early in the gathering gloom and flickering in the falling snow, announced their arrival.

John Ogilvie was much younger than Pauline had expected. Around thirty-five and clearly worried. His expression was grief-stricken. Alan introduced them and they sat in the office waiting area to talk.

"When Frank said he'd asked you to look into this, I had no idea who you were, Miss Riddell. My office deals only with civil matters so criminal investigations aren't part of our world. I'm told you have solved many difficult cases; I hope you can help us too. What can I tell you," Ogilvie said, "that will help you understand the situation?"

"Start by telling me about when the will was made and how it has been kept."

"The will is little more than an update to the will that

Frank's dad inherited from. In fact, apart from the names and some changes to incorporate new legal terms, the will hasn't changed since the eighteenth century. The eldest son gets the estate and siblings get allowances. In the present family, there is only one surviving sibling and that's Anthony."

"So, the will was changed recently?" Pauline asked.

"Oh no, not recently. Shortly after the death of the original heir, Peter. He was killed in the war, so the changes happened in 1945."

"You weren't working here then," Pauline said.

Ogilvie shook his head. "I was still at school. My father and his clerk, Harry Teesdale, made the changes and the will was signed and locked in our archives, where it has been until I got it out about a week ago when I heard old Mr. Thornton was not going to survive very much longer. That's when I found it didn't say what it should say."

"What does Harry Teesdale say about the will? Surely he remembers what was written?"

"Unfortunately, Harry is dead. When my father retired from the business, old Harry retired too. That was about five years ago. He went off to live in Spain where I'm afraid he died only a year later."

"Did he have relatives in Spain?"

"No, nothing like that. He was a bachelor who rarely traveled so I suppose he saved much of his salary. Anyway, he purchased a house there later in life and spent his summer holidays in it for a number of years. When he retired, he sold his home here and moved to Spain, which he said was better for his rheumatism."

Pauline nodded but didn't point out what Ogilvie, as a lawyer, must know. Spain had no extradition treaty with the United Kingdom. If 'old Harry' switched the will, he couldn't have been brought to trial for it. This was more like a how-to-prove-the-will-a-forgery case, than a 'who dun it'. "Was his death unexpected?" she asked.

Grab your copy...
vinci-books.com/murderforchristmas

About the Author

I've always loved mysteries, especially those involving Agatha Christie's Miss Marple. Perhaps because Miss Marple reminded me of my aunts when I was growing up. But Agatha never told us much about Miss Marple's earlier life. While writing my own elderly super-sleuth series, I'm tracing her career from the start. As you'll see, if you follow the Miss Riddell Cozy Mysteries over the coming years.

However, this is my Bio, not Miss Riddell's, so here goes with all you need to know about me: After retiring, I became a writer and when I'm not working on the computer, you'll find me running, cycling, walking, and taking wildlife photos wherever and whenever I can.

My cozy mystery series begins in northern England because that was my home growing up and that's also the home of so many great cozy mysteries. Stay with me though because Miss Riddell loves to travel as much as I do and the stories will take us to many different places around the world.

Acknowledgments

I'd like to thank my editors, illustrator and the many others who have helped with this book. Without them, my books would look very sorry indeed.

www.ingramcontent.com/pod-product-compliance
Lightning Source LLC
Chambersburg PA
CBHW011347010726
47493CB00011B/2987